HOPE LIKE HELL

Miranda Sapphire

For my own Maggie—I wish I could have helped more.

And for all the weirdos who think that something is wrong with them;
you're suffering from a defect of place, not a defect of self

* * *

Blurb: Eva is a single mother struggling to make ends meet and raise her daughter right. She doesn't have time for dating, but Seth manages to waltz into her life and sweep her off her feet with his smoldering good looks and effortless charm. Yet Seth isn't what he seems (he's secretly an alien, for one) and they'll have to hope like hell they can make it work—because walking away might not be an option.

Content Warnings: transphobia, bullying of a minor, assault of a trans minor, graphic descriptions of a skin condition that causes boils and lesions, discussion of human trafficking, hypothetical child abduction, sexual harassment, panic attacks happening on-page, graphic sex scenes, adult language.

Tropes: MF, fated mates, single mother, short king, ND FMC, reformed bad boy who is actually a cinnamon roll, aliens among us, found family.

Chapter 1

Riff Raff, Street Rat

<u>SEPHYR</u>

It was always the same: I was laughing, wrapped in golden warmth in the backseat of my parent's hover. My mother's tinkling laughter underscored my father's harsh barks, making a melody more perfect than I'd ever been able to find in music. It was dark, nighttime, but it didn't feel dark.

Not yet.

I never knew what they were laughing about, only that at some point in the dream it always became cruel, a mockery of happiness instead of the happiness itself. It heralded in the moment when everything changed, when blaring bright light tore through the snuggling dark, ripping through that cocoon of laughter and cutting my parents' lives far too short.

I jolted awake, my breath stuck in my throat and my heart hammering in my chest. Cold sweat soaked my sheets, sticking them to my skin and fur, but it was the insistent ringing of my wristcom, letting me know I had a call incoming, that made me feel the most uncomfortable. According to the display, it was the last person I wanted to talk to after that particular dream: my employer, notorious head of the th'rak brotherhood, Serr'eza. I scrubbed a hand roughly over my face and tried to finger-comb my hair into looking halfway presentable, my third eye sliding closed with lingering fatigue. I flicked accept on the flashing holographic display, forcing my expression neutral.

"What is it, Serr'eza?"

"Always a pleasure talking to you, too, Kasdaan." The biolights suspended in Serr'eza's translucent red flesh flashed angrily, showing his displeasure where a lack of a mouth and beady all-black eyes failed. "If you're done showing your poor breeding, I have important things to get to today, so…"

"Yeah, fuck you too, buddy. I was sleeping, so let's hurry this along so I can get back to dreaming about taking three beautiful females at once instead of looking at your ugly mug."

Serr'eza snarled, his lights flaring bright, but it was all a part of the game with guys like him; he got to the point. "I have several buyers lined up for the next shipment and want you planetside. You've had weeks to get your recon done and I'm sick of paying you to sit on your ass—"

"You're *not* paying me though, asshole. I'm doing you a *favor*—"

"So that your debts with the brotherhood can be wiped clean. Fucking *vrakaashaad.*"

I rolled my eyes so that he could see. "Look, there's a reason why this takes a while, and picking up where a dead male left off on an operation this complex—with no notes on where he was at in the process, I might add—is going to take even *more* time than usual. But I'm just about there; all I need's another couple of days in orbit to flesh out my assumed ID and I'll be ready." Serr'eza clearly had no idea what kind of care it took to infiltrate someplace without being detected.

There was no room to wing it; not blending in with the natives was how you got caught. And as impatient as Serr'eza was to dive in, I knew that he also wanted things done right so that the Collective Space Enforcers had no reason to come calling. "We done here?"

Serr'eza's beady black eyes narrowed so far that they damn near disappeared. "Tread lightly, Kasdaan. You talk a big game but you know what happens if you don't deliver on time. If my clients are unhappy, I'm *very* unhappy. And ain't no one in the universe gonna come looking for you if you disappear." The call cut out as abruptly as it had come in, leaving me alone and deeply uncomfortable.

Serr'eza was a bastard, no question, but he wasn't exactly *wrong*, and that hurt more than a 24-year-old wound should. I lay there in my bunk, willing my mind not to replay that one moment that flavored my every nightmare…and failing. I saw the bright light that proceeded the collision again and again, heard the earsplitting crash of metal and glass shattering, the molten pieces slicing through the only two people I'd had in the world like a lasknife. I heard their screams on a loop, and then I heard the terrible silence that had settled in when those screams had stopped, and it was just me, alone and sobbing.

I groaned, barking out the command for the daylights to switch on and swinging my legs over the edge of the cot. I scratched idly at the huge twisted scar that trailed from shoulder to elbow on my right arm—the one I'd gotten in that accident when I was just four. I peeled off my still-damp clothes, getting ready to head into the cleaning stall, when another, far worse klaxon started up.

Proximity alarm. And all the way out here, that only

meant one thing: trouble. I swore, pulling up the video feed for the triggered alarm on my wristcom and swearing more emphatically when I saw "Collective Space Enforcement" emblazoned on the side of the vehicle headed my way. I had minutes to get my little ship planetside before they'd be on me —they'd tripped the sensor I'd stationed on Earth's only moon, luckily, or else I'd probably already be boarded.

I dove through the cramped hallway in just my underwear and flew into the pilot's chair, taking the lithe stealth ship the brotherhood was lending me for this job out of sleep mode and throwing her into motion. I didn't have to worry about the humans picking me up on their monitoring systems, since my cloak outclassed anything they had down there, but a Collective ship would be able to make quick work of it and find me out.

I tipped her nose down and dove straight for the landmass I'd been staying above while I'd absorbed hours of holos and books and entertainment media in preparation for my stay on this strange little planet. They called it the United States, or more commonly just the initials US, and I was confident that I'd gotten enough of a feel for their culture to be able to fake being human. But having to dodge Collective enforcers meant I'd have to craft my Earth credentials *fast*.

I was hovering over Lake Michigan when I finally pulled out of my descent, my heart once again racing and cold sweat coating my skin. I spotted strange structures on the horizon, and a quick search of the planet's positioning system revealed I was just offshore from an entertainment park called "Navy Pier" in the midwestern city of Chicago. I'd considered it and several other large cities for my base of operations, so after a moment of consideration I decided I'd settle here. I fired up the powerful computer array the brotherhood had installed into the ship for fabricating documents and hacking into secure systems and got to work.

Luckily the human's version of a nexus, which they called "the internet", was almost laughably easy to break into and insert the documentation I'd need to pass as a citizen. I threw something together as quick as I could and snatched up a house that would serve my purposes, pilfering several hundred thousand credits—no, *dollars*, I'd need to get used to that—from big companies who wouldn't miss them. When I was done only about an hour had passed while I hovered over the filthy lake. It wasn't my best work, but it would have to do.

As far as anyone on Earth would ever know, I was now Seth Meyers, a 28-year-old Chicago native who worked as a contract security guard, with parents living just outside of Indianapolis and a sister down in Florida. If I was going to create a fake life for myself, might as well make it nice and cozy, right?

From there all that was left to do was to generate the skin my helix cranial implant would produce to disguise me as a human. Since I didn't know how long I'd be planetside, I kept it as close to my actual appearance as I could; I wouldn't be able to get more nanos here if my helix ran low, so the less my helix had to completely obscure with its nanobot mesh, the better.

I checked the look of it in the mirror in the hygiene room, feeling *real* weird about what I saw. It was still my short, coppery hair, the curls shaved down almost to the scalp except on the top, where I liked it a little longer to hide the tiny vestigial ears I'd gotten from my felican mother. No one on

Earth had tusks or fangs or a third eye, so those were hidden —all a gift from my yvrenii father—but the olive tone of my skin had been close enough to some human colorations that I'd kept that. Tattoos and piercings were also common enough on Earth, so I hadn't needed to hide those, either. Thanks to Dad my tail was just a little stub of a thing instead of the long furry appendage most full-blooded felicans had, a fact which I was immensely grateful for as I considered just how many nanos that was probably saving me.

It was strange to see myself as a human male, to see all of the things I'd spent the last 28 years of my life thinking of as "my face" suddenly erased, but that was true anytime I wore a helix skin. This time I was struck by how making myself human had also somehow made me…cohesive.

There weren't many people like me in the Collective—hybrids from parents belonging to two completely different-looking species. But during the brief time I'd known them it had been clear they'd been a true mate pair, genuinely in love, and they'd been crazy about me.

Too bad about the accident though, because aside from them, *nobody* had wanted me—I wasn't yvrenii enough for other yvrenii, I was *too* yvrenii for the felicans, and no one else wanted to deal with such a strange-looking kid. I drew a lot of attention being what I was, and in a lot of the homes I'd stayed in—too many to count in the fourteen years getting cycled through the foster care system—getting attention was the last thing they needed.

But being what I was had also made me really good at this line of work; I'd spent my whole young life becoming a shapeshifter: someone who could take a look at a group and figure out exactly how they'd need to look and act for them to get ignored. Which was the ideal state—a lot of people thought you needed to be popular to fit in, but being in the background was far safer and more sustainable.

Satisfied with my slapdash ID and needing to get to proper cover before the enforcers pinged me, I took my cloaked ship back up into the air and guided it carefully to the property I was now in possession of, a modest bungalow on the near northwest side. I'd get settled in, put up the more powerful cloaking fields in the garage so that the Collective agents wouldn't be able to find me if they decided to linger in orbit, and then get to work.

I was going to open an orphanage in the name of the brotherhood. And then they'd have a steady stream of kids they could take off-world and sell to the wealthy *vrakaashaad* who wanted them. Or at least, that was what Serr'eza had sent me here to do. But if I played everything right, what I'd actually be doing was escaping the whole mess. Find a nice Earth female and marry her, destroy anything the brotherhood could use to track me, and go dark. I was tired of always looking over my shoulder, and they were crazy if they thought I'd help them kidnap innocent kids for their sick business.

I found my new home, touching down in the backyard for now, and took a second to admire it. "Home sweet home," I murmured to myself, something like hope filling my chest for the first time in far too long.

Chapter 2

Don't Panic

"Magdalena Nadzija, if you don't get up *right now* you'll be late!" I called from outside my fourteen-year-old daughter's bedroom. I felt for her, I really did, because I remembered how hard it had been to get up for school when I was her age, but I was running late for work on top of her being tardy too much lately, and my frustration had leaked into my voice.

I heard a groan from the other side of the door, and then some hard smacks as Maggie flung her covers off with every ounce of teenage rage in her body. "I'm up!" she snapped, and I couldn't help smiling at what an absolute *teen* she was sometimes.

"Thank you, monkey!"

I double-checked that I'd gotten her food for the day all packed up and waiting for her on the console table by the front door, then went to the kitchen to finish up my own breakfast and finish checking my emails. I wasn't technically on the clock yet, but my boss, Phil, liked me to start taking calls right when my shift started, and as much as I hated this job I also needed it, so I'd gotten into the habit of checking my messages first thing in the morning. It was a good job in that it was better about being flexible with my hours than other places had been. It was just me and Maggie in my little family, so being able to move my shift around to take her to school or go to parent-teacher meetings was essential. It just wasn't the kind of work I wanted to be doing, and the pay was only good if I could scrape up some overtime, which lost it some points, too.

I finished the last couple of lukewarm sips of my coffee and shoved a banana in my mouth—most of the bunch was getting a little too brown, but that just meant I'd be able to make banana bread this weekend—and finished reading through my work emails. Then I slipped into the bathroom, checking that the bandage in my armpit hadn't moved when I'd gotten dressed. That was the reason I was running late—I was fighting a nasty hidradenitis suppurativa flare-up and had woken up with my armpit crusted with blood.

This flare-up was extra irritating because I'd been able to find some dietary changes that had put it into remission for the last several years, but something must have changed recently to bring it roaring back. Still more infuriatingly, it was now cropping up in different places from where I was used to getting it. You develop a kind of system for dealing with things like that, and suddenly getting them in my armpit when I was used to getting them in my bikini zone was really throwing me.

Once I was satisfied my clothes were indeed safe from this flare-up of my autoimmune disorder I returned to the kitchen to try for another cup of coffee before I had to leave to take Maggie.

The bathroom door slammed just as my phone started buzzing next to me on the table. I glanced at the screen and let out a groan—it was Phil. He never wanted anything good before noon.

"Good morning, Phil," I chirped, dread making my stomach sour.

"Eva, I have some bad news, I'm afraid. Corporate had a big budget meeting yesterday and unfortunately, we're going to have to cut hours across the board. The most I can do is thirty a week now for our current staff of customer service reps."

I wanted to scream, to cry, but I took a deep breath and let it out slowly, trying my best to get myself under control. "Oh. Um, okay, thanks for letting me know," I heard myself say brightly. "If there's any changes please let me know. Shifts I can pick up or overtime I could do." Despair sank its teeth in and threatened to swallow me up. There was no way I'd be able to make ends meet on just the income from thirty hours. I'd have to get a second job, maybe even find a smaller but more affordable place to move into. *What am I going to do?* I thought, feeling small and helplessly adrift.

"Sure thing, thanks for being so understanding, Eva," he said before giving me a hasty goodbye and disconnecting the call.

I took some deep breaths, needing to get control of myself before Maggie was done getting ready. It didn't do any good to freak out about it now, when she'd see and worry about me. It already seemed like she carried the weight of the world on her slim shoulders, and I was desperate not to make anything in my life her burden.

My daughter shuffled into the kitchen, bleary-eyed and looking extremely grumpy, but she managed a half-hearted smile for me. "Alright, I'm ready," she intoned, gesturing at her all-black outfit and heavily lined eyes. I managed a smile back, snatching my phone off the table.

"Excellent; then let's get going, my love."

She nodded, following me to the entryway and snagging all of her stuff where I'd piled it. I grabbed my cardigan from its hook and nudged her out the door so that I could lock it behind us.

Maggie let out a jaw-cracking yawn as she slumped into the front passenger seat, her gray eyes, just like mine, glazed and unfocused. I frowned at how tired she was. Was she *too* tired? I felt my chest tighten with worry. I'd have to remember to talk to her later, check in with her and make sure she was doing okay. My throat started to feel tight, my heart rate creeping higher as I looked at the light of my life and my mind raced with all the ways I could be letting her down.

My chest remained tight the entire drive to Maggie's school, my breaths just a little bit too shallow. I tried to engage Maggie in conversation, as much to distract myself as to try and figure out what was going on with her, but all she did was grunt and give me one-word answers, so I left her alone.

We were one of the last cars to pull up in the drop-off lane at her school, but the first bell hadn't quite rung yet. "You have your backpack? Your food?" I asked as she gathered herself to start heading inside.

She nodded. "Yeah, Mom."

"Good." I leaned over and pressed a kiss to her cheek, relishing the whiff of her scent I caught, that hint of something that made me think of when she was a baby and I'd just sit there huffing her smell for hours. "Love you," I told her, giving her my best smile even as my heart felt like it was going to race right out of my chest. "Have a great day! I'll see you later."

"Love you too, Mom," she mumbled, turning and leaving me with a wave as the first bell rang out. I watched her retreating back for a second, then pulled away from the curb and started heading home.

My chest was still feeling strange and tight, and now that Maggie was out of the car and I was alone it felt like it was getting worse. I tried to clear my throat, smacking my palm against my sternum; it felt almost like there was something stuck in there, something that ached and throbbed across my whole chest. My airway was feeling tighter now, and I was starting to feel hot and cold at the same time, my pulse throbbing way too hard.

When my vision started to blacken at the edges I adjusted my course to go to the hospital instead of home. Something felt wrong, felt *really* wrong, and it was starting to scare me.

By the time I pulled up in front of the emergency room I was barely breathing, my lungs starved for air. Was this a heart attack? I was barely thirty-five; I *couldn't* be having a heart attack, could I?

I made it past the doors and was almost at the front desk when my weak knees gave out and everything went dark.

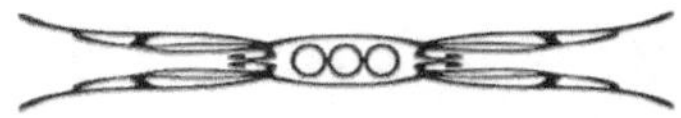

"A panic attack?" I asked incredulously.

The nurse nodded, her salt and pepper hair pulled back into a low ponytail. "Yes, honey. We did an EKG and a cardiac workup just in case and everything looked good." She peered over the tops of her pink cat-eye glasses at me. "Was this your first one?"

I nodded, speechless. All of that and it was just a panic attack?

The nurse smiled at me, clasping my shoulder in one warm hand. "Panic attacks are no joke, sweetie," she said gently, reading my mind. "Most people agree it feels like a heart attack, especially if you've never had one before and you don't know what it is."

All I could do was keep nodding and try not to look like I was as close to bursting into tears as I actually was. I was late for work (and Phil was furious) for *this*? I felt so stupid and pathetic.

"You should really see someone about your stress," the nurse added, moving to the computer to add things to my chart. "You keep pushing yourself too hard and you could wind up with a real heart attack. Stress leads to heart disease, and heart disease is one of the top killers of women. I don't want to scare you, but it's serious stuff."

She handed me my discharge papers and a prescription for Prozac, then told me I was free to go.

I wanted to crawl into a hole and disappear, but I really needed to get to work. If I worked through lunch it wouldn't be too bad, though. I tried to save my PTO for when Mags was sick, so I could take care of her without having to worry about working it into my schedule or dividing my attention, and if I skipped lunch I'd only have to use a half hour. That way I'd still be able to spend as much time as I needed this evening having a heart-to-heart with my girl.

I sighed, pushing my dark brown hair out of my eyes. It wasn't worth it to spend the money on the drugs, so I tossed the prescription in the recycling as soon as I got home. Maggie needed her HRT more, and I could try and do some breathing exercises the next time it happened to cut it off at the pass. I'd be fine.

Chapter 3

Meet Weird

<u>SEPHYR</u>

Sandra had been the third female I'd met with on a date since I'd settled into my bungalow in the northwestern Chicago suburbs four weeks ago, and while she'd been nice she'd also been distant—like all of the females had been so far.

It had started off well enough: I'd met her at a restaurant, something casual but quiet with good food. We'd had nice conversations through the dating app I'd used to find her, and I was hopeful that the date would go well. But something just didn't click in person. Her interests hadn't quite lined up with mine, and our conversation had quickly become flat and boring.

"I'm sorry, Seth," she'd apologized at the end of the meal, "it's just that I...I don't think you and I would be a good fit."

"Yeah, I get it. Thanks for coming out to see me at least." I was disappointed, but truth be told I hadn't felt much of a connection, either. Sure, I wanted to find a female to date to help my cover, but I wasn't in such a rush that I had to settle for someone that I didn't really mesh with. I could still disappear and hide from the brotherhood as a human even if I was a single male.

If I was going to go to the trouble of dating a human and having to hide the fact that I wasn't human myself, I wanted there to at least be a real connection. Someone who liked the shows and movies I'd grown fond of while I was developing my understanding of Earth culture and mannerisms. I wanted to be able to discuss the Earth books I liked—especially the "comics" they'd invented here, which blended books and art into a thrilling combination that had blown my mind when I first encountered it.

Even if we'd ended things amicably, I was still feeling a little down about myself and lonely after my rejections, and that meant I'd wound up at my favorite food shop. I meandered past the aisles of the Save-n-Shop, heading for the frozen section at the back of the store. I felt the urge to purchase and consume several of the specialty ice cream pints that were one of the truly great things about Earth shops such as this.

I stood in front of the frosty glass doors, my hands on my hips as I considered the variety of tantalizing flavors on display. I loved how refreshing the mint chocolate chip was, but peanut butter cup also sounded delightful. Then there was cookie dough, whose tiny balls of chewy dough were so good I could never get enough. The Save-n-Shop was running a sale, buy one get one half off, so I could get four for the price of three…

I became aware of labored breathing an aisle over, my keen yvrenii ears also noting something like a whine. My brow furrowed, and I cocked my head, going still to try and hear better.

Yes, there was definitely someone struggling to breathe nearby, in distress, and as much as I didn't want to interfere and risk having to talk to the authorities, I could neither hear nor scent anyone else nearby. I didn't want to draw attention to myself, but with no one else around to help, how could I not step in? If the police needed to be called I'd just have to slip away somehow.

When I rounded the corner I saw a lone human woman sunk into a deep squat on the floor, her hands clutching her throat like she couldn't breathe, a basket tipped over beside her, and several frozen items scattered around her on the floor. I couldn't see her face, her dark brown hair having fallen forward to cover it.

I approached her slowly, not wanting to startle her. "Are you alright?" I asked, crouching down to her height once I was close. "Should I get someone?"

She sucked in a rough, shuddering breath and looked up at me with wide gray eyes glazed with tears.

"No!" she gasped, her mouth open like a dying fish. "Please."

She started wheezing, her fingers digging into her throat. She was clearly having trouble breathing, but aside from being a little pale, her color was good.

There was something about this that was familiar to me, but it took me a moment to place it. "Panic attack?" I asked softly, recognizing the signs from when the damn things had plagued me in my early teens.

She looked at me, her brow furrowed like she was confused or she couldn't answer me.

I spotted a bag of frozen peas in the pile of spilled groceries and grabbed it before shuffling a little closer to her. I put the bag in the middle of my chest, demonstrating. "Can you put this on your chest just like this for me?"

Her hand loosened from her throat, confusion settling into her pretty features, but she took the bag from me and did what I'd told her. "Good, there you go. Now, I know it feels like you can't breathe but I promise you, you can. I want you to breathe with me, okay?" She nodded, tears trailing down her face as she gasped.

"You're alright," I promised her. "Breathe in..." I breathed in slowly to a count of four, "Hold it for two. Good, now out for four, and hold for two." She did her best to mimic me, though she was still definitely struggling. "Alright, now we do it again. Here we go..." I guided her through several more cycles, until it seemed like she was able to control her breathing again and her tears had stopped falling.

Now that I was looking at her more closely, I was realizing that she was *quite* lovely. Her face was wide and open, with large gray eyes and thick dark eyebrows. Her nose was long and hooked and gave her face a regal air. She had a delicate, pointed chin, like the mythical fairies so many human stories revolved around. There was something about her that made me want to reach out and touch her, even though we were strangers. But I couldn't stop the smile that curled my lips at seeing her calm.

"There you are," I murmured. "Told you you were alright."

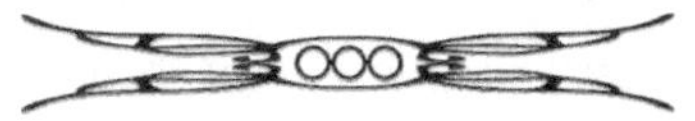

EVA

I was dimly aware of someone helping me, soothing me, while my mind spiraled out of control and my heart felt like it was trying to burst out of my chest, but it didn't really register that it was a stranger, a man, until I'd begun to calm down enough to get air.

And then I realized I was face to face with quite possibly the most attractive person I'd ever seen, and I felt immediately dumpy and embarrassed. This extremely handsome man was smiling at me gently, making the piercing underneath his full bottom lip sparkle in the harsh lighting of the grocery store.

"There you are," he said, his voice raspy and deep but still kind, still gentle. "How're you feeling?" He had a bit of an accent I couldn't quite place, a Southern twang colored by something that might have been European, and hearing it directed at me with such sweetness was having an incredibly strong reaction on me.

"I'm...I'm alright. I think. I—um, thank you." My voice sounded squeaky and breathless. Some of it was the lingering effects of the panic attack, but too much of it was his shocking gold eyes and square jaw, was the way his boyish curls of coppery hair contrasted with his tattoos and piercings. He was big, too; even crouched down his body was enormous, his forearms corded with muscle, his shoulders broad and thighs thick, and after fourteen years without any urge to date I was suddenly *very* interested.

What great timing, huh?

"You're very welcome," he told me, holding his hand out for me to shake. "I'm Seth. Nice to meet you..."

"Eva," I responded, taking his hand. His skin was so warm, and just the right amount of rough from callouses. It was hard for me to let it go.

"Oh my god, *Mom*? What happened, are you alright?!" I winced, then turned around and did my best to smile at my daughter like nothing was wrong, like I hadn't just had a panic attack in the middle of the grocery store while she'd gone to use the bathroom.

"Um, yes! Yes, I'm fine. Just um—" I scrambled. "I just had a dizzy spell. It's nothing, I promise."

I realized it was a mistake to say that as soon as the words were out. Maggie's face blanched, worry pinching her brows —the mirror of mine, thick and dark. "A-are you sick? Should I call an ambulance?" She must have finally noticed Seth behind me, because her eyes narrowed and her lips dipped into a frown. "And who the fuck are you?" she snapped, "You perving on my mom, asshole?"

I let out an indignant squawk. "Maggie! Language!" I turned to Seth to apologize, but to my surprise he was smiling at her, looking impressed.

"Is this your bodyguard, Eva?" he asked me, those golden eyes looking amused instead of angry. "She's very fierce."

Maggie narrowed her eyes at him, looking as intimidating as a gangly fourteen-year-old alt kid could.

"My name's Seth," he introduced himself, standing and holding that huge hand out to my daughter. "I was just around the corner when your mom started not feeling good and I tried to help." His full lips were quirked up in a little smile, like he liked my daughter's antics and found her endearing. Which would be a first. Mags was...difficult with new people. Being trans meant her guard was always up, and she came across prickly to most people. With the way things were in this country right now, I really couldn't blame her, and it wasn't like I was Ms. Social Butterfly, myself.

I got to my feet and smiled at my daughter again. "It's fine, baby. Really. He was just helping." I turned back to Seth, taking in just how broad and muscular he was now that we were both standing. He'd look intimidating if it wasn't for his kind eyes and soft smile. It also helped that he wasn't towering over me, us being the same height.

Maggie's shoulders relaxed just a fraction. "Whatever. Are you really okay, Mom? Maybe you should go to the hospital."

I grimaced. I hadn't wanted to tell her I was having panic attacks now, didn't want her to worry or think that I wasn't able to take care of her, but it felt like if I didn't come clean this was going to spiral quickly. "It's not an illness. It was just, um...a panic attack. I'm fine now, really!"

The look of guilt and devastation on her face surprised me. "Since when do you have panic attacks?" she asked me quietly.

"Since today," I admitted, trying to chuckle like it was nothing. Because it was—I wasn't dying or anything, I was just doing a bad job of managing my stress. "I really am fine, sweetie."

Maggie gulped, Seth seemingly forgotten for the moment. "What triggered it?" she asked me.

My face went hot. "Nothing you need to worry about. Everything's alright, I promise." I felt so stupid now, letting myself get worked up because the ready meals we relied on during the week had shot up in price by fifty cents—along with a lot of our other staples gradually creeping up in cost. If I had to get a second job to let us keep our quality of life then I'd just have to suck it up and do it. At least Maggie was older now and wouldn't need a babysitter.

"Panic attacks won't kill you, but they're not nothing," Seth said quietly, and both me and Maggie turned to him, surprised.

"Thank you, yes! Mom, it is totally serious!" Maggie

exclaimed, throwing her arms out. "And it kind of hurts my feelings that you think I'm too stupid to know that," she added more softly.

I swallowed, throat feeling thick. "It's not that; I don't think you're stupid *at all*. If anything I think you're too smart for your own good." I reached out for her, taking her hand and pulling her into a one-armed hug. "If anything I'm the dummy for thinking I could get anything past you." I kissed her temple and released her.

I'd half forgotten about him, but Seth was still standing there, something in his expression that I couldn't quite read.

I cleared my throat, hugging myself as I turned to him. "Thank you," I told him, surprised by how much I meant it. I didn't like people getting in my business like that, but if Maggie had been the one to stumble on me instead of him, when I was stuck in the thick of it, I didn't even want to imagine how much that might have upset her. "I—I'd like to do something to thank you. You didn't have to help me like that and it was really…kind."

He looked surprised, but a warm grin quickly took its place. "It was my pleasure," he said, looking like he meant it. "If it's not too presumptuous…I'd like you to thank me by letting me take you out to dinner."

Wow, hadn't seen that one coming.

"I thought you said you weren't perving on her, asshat," Maggie interjected, though with much less venom than last time.

"Hey, be nice," I chided, poking her gently in the ribs.

Seth chuckled, rubbing at the back of his neck. "I know. But I can't help that it started off as innocently wanting to help but ended up with me realizing just how pretty your mom is." He smiled at me, looking a little uncertain, for all his boldness.

She stared him down for several seconds, then seemed to decide he wasn't an immediate threat.

"Alright. I'll allow it. But you better watch yourself."

I laughed, looking between the two of them. "Hey, hi, hello, I think you two forgot I was here and that I need to have a say in this." Maggie twisted her mouth, giving me her sorry face.

"I don't want you to feel uncomfortable, Eva," Seth interjected, his voice gentle yet earnest. "You don't need to agree to anything. I swear, just being able to help and hearing thanks is plenty."

I took a second to try and examine the situation. He knew I had a teenage daughter, that I was apparently the sort of person who had panic attacks—and in public, no less—and what I looked like without makeup on and halfway into my pajamas, and yet he was somehow still interested.

Maybe he was crazy. Or trying to grift me.

But there was also a chance, however unlikely in my mind, that he was being genuine. I had a hard time reading situations sometimes, but usually I could at least trust my gut to tell me if a person was cool or not. And nothing about Seth so far was setting off alarm bells.

And then there was the fact that I hadn't dated anyone since Maggie was conceived. I didn't have time to date now that I'd probably have to get a second job, but on the other hand, if I could secure a partner, that would take away some of my burdens. I'd have someone besides my teenage daughter to turn to.

"Okay," I said, biting my lip. "What did you have in

mind?"

He beamed at me, looking like he'd won some huge prize. "You guys like pizza? There's this place nearby here called Leonie's if you're interested."

Before I could say anything, Maggie interjected, answering for me. "Oh yeah, she is definitely interested. Give him your number, Mom!"

I laughed, pulling her into another half-hug. "Magdalena Nadzija, I swear to god, you and your pizza lust are going to get us killed one day."

"What?!" she cried, giggling. "You're going to turn down free pizza?"

"No, honey, *I'm* the one getting the pizza, because Seth was so nice in helping me—"

"Uh, actually I was planning on treating you. In the interest of full disclosure."

I turned to look at him, my brow deeply furrowed in confusion. "Wait, what?"

Maggie rolled her eyes, pointing at Seth. "He thinks you're cute. He wants to take you out on a date. You agreeing to go out with him is the payback."

Seth grinned, bowing his head at her. "Thank you for the clarification, ma'am," he told her. That got her to smile— actually *smile*—and that made me melt just a little bit more. I was a little thrown by just how fast she'd shifted from standoffish to friendly, but that had to be a good sign, right? Like when you brought someone home and your pet immediately liked them?

She turned back to me, a glint in her eye that usually meant I was about to have my hands full. "I like him. You should definitely date him."

"Is that so?" I scoffed.

"Especially if he's also going to buy me pizza." She looked over at Seth with a very obvious *well?* sort of expression.

"Absolutely. I'd love to take both of you out. Can I give you my number?" he asked me, his eyes warm and lips quirked up in amusement.

I blinked at him. Before I could stop myself, I blurted, "Why?"

Seth took a half step closer, licking his lips. "What do you mean, why?"

"She's shy," Maggie interrupted, throwing one of her arms around my waist and urging me closer. "She doesn't think she's a catch, so you're going to have to work at convincing her." My sputtering went ignored.

Seth grinned. "I can do that," he said quietly, looking at me like he really did mean it. My heart started hammering in my chest, heat pooling low in my belly.

"Alright," I breathed, holding out my hand before I could change my mind. He handed me his phone with the text app opened, and I sent myself a text to get his number. My phone pinged in my purse, and he grinned.

"'preciate it, Eva," he said, that sinfully sexy grin still plastered on his face. "I'll talk to you later, then. You have a nice night, ladies." Then he was walking away with one last wave.

I gathered up the rest of our spilled groceries and started heading towards the front check-out. Once we were in line, I turned to Maggie, frowning in concentration. "Was that weird?"

She shrugged, cleaning under her nails. "I don't know. Possibly. But he seemed nice and he *is* feeding us so…"

I snorted. "You have a one-track mind, love." After a moment I added. "Did he pass the vibe check, then?"

She considered. "Yeah, I think so. He didn't seem sus to me."

I nodded, biting my lip as I turned from her and started piling our purchases on the line. "Did you like him?"

"Meh. You talked to him more than me. But I like that he likes you," Maggie told me, leaning her head on my arm when I paused. I absolutely loved that about her: she was sarcastic and even a little caustic, but so sweet and loving once she trusted you, and if you managed to win her loyalty she'd go to the ends of the earth. I didn't know how to handle her sometimes, but getting to be her mom was the greatest joy and honor I thought I could ever possibly receive.

"I love you, monkey," I murmured into her hair, kissing her temple as we waited for our things to get rung up.

"I love you, too, Mom." After a moment, she added, "Please don't hide things like the panic attacks from me. I know you're trying to protect me, but even if you hide it I still know something's wrong, and it drives me crazy."

Guilt knifed through me. "I'm sorry. I just don't want you to think you're responsible for my feelings. You're still a kid and I have *every* intention of letting you stay that way." We fell silent, Maggie "sneaking" two packs of her favorite mint-berry gum onto the belt at the very end like she always did.

Chapter 4

Taking the Low Road

<u>SEPHYR</u>

Fuck me.

Still not sure what happened back there, but as odd as it had been I couldn't honestly say I regretted it.

I'd seen Eva curled up and in pain, and it was all instinct from there: swooping in, calming her down, making sure she was safe and well. I hadn't been able to stop myself, and that had me a little worried—control had always been the difference between life and death for me, and I hadn't survived this long by letting mine slip.

Where other young males in the homes I'd lived in had let themselves get riled up and territorial, I'd just walked away. They could call me whatever they wanted; once I realized that keeping a hold on my temper meant the difference between a night in lockup and staying free it was an easy choice. And as I'd gotten older, and the fights had gotten bloodier, keeping cool meant I saw the blow coming, meant I could think things through and wriggle out of tough situations when the people around me were flailing and rage blind.

I shook my head, unlocking my car with a beep and folding myself into the front seat. I started the engine and pulled out of the parking lot, heading home.

It wasn't until I was pulling up out front that I realized I hadn't bought that ice cream after all. I hadn't bought *anything* after running into Eva and Maggie. For some reason, that made me smile.

I dug my phone out of my pocket and pulled up my texts. I composed a new one and sent it to the only real contact in my address book, Eva:

Me: Hope you two made it home safe. How soon is too soon to set up that dinner?

I locked the screen and got out of my car, deactivating my alarm with my helix via neural command before slipping into the side door. I headed upstairs to my room for a shower and to finally take the damn helix skin off, to let my body breathe.

Once I was in my room and certain that all of the windows were properly cloaked I disabled the skin with another neural command. A relieved groan ripped from my throat as it dissolved, fresh air touching me directly for the first time all day.

My skin was dewed with sweat, making my coppery fur cling to it where it grew on my limbs, lower torso, and back. My stub of a tail, finally freed from my pants, twitched in the air. But possibly the biggest relief was getting full use of my third eye again—while I was in the skin things were largely obscured, not quite dark but dim and very badly blurred, since that part of my face had to look blank, and it drove me fucking *nuts*.

I hopped in the shower, feeling jittery and strange. I'd thought it was the strain of wearing the skin for so long, but now that I was out of it the feeling hadn't faded. What was going on with me? I just had to hope this wouldn't distract me while I strung Serr'eza along and prepared to go to ground. Distractions were dangerous.

I fingered the tangled puckers of scar tissue peppering my skin, remembering how they'd wound up mine. My skin was a tapestry of proof that it didn't do to get distracted.

The deep, rough groove that traced the bottom edge of my ribs from front to back had been from my first "boss", a pimply teenaged yvrenii named Kus who'd had me steal some food and then tried to kill me so he wouldn't have to split the haul. I'd managed to twist at the last second so he didn't get any vital organs, but it still ached sometimes. Up until then, I'd considered him my brother.

Then there was the necklace of pale shiny scars around my throat from when a bounty I'd been trying to collect had tried to garrote me. I'd followed him into a dimly lit club, and just a second of watching the band play had been all the opportunity he'd needed. Lucky for me he'd thought I was pure felican 'cause of the fur and the vestigial ears on the top of my head, but I had the thick protective cartilage plates running under the skin of my throat from my yvrenii father, and I'd managed to reach back and shoot him in the face before he figured it out. It had been a good payday at least, even though it'd been worth less with him dead.

My fingers found the twisted knot on my right hip, remembering the gorgeous felican female who'd given it to me. She'd been stunning, all gleaming russet fur and long lithe limbs, and when she'd sought me out in that bar and started flirting with me I couldn't believe my luck. She'd taken me by the hand and dragged me out into the alley, getting down on her knees on the wet concrete and pulling my cock out of my pants so fast it made my head spin. There was just enough light for me to spot the small blaster she pulled out of a thigh holster and redirect the shot so it glanced off my hip.

I clenched my jaw, dropping my hands from my body and snatching the shampoo off its shelf. The past was a useful tool, but it didn't do to dwell on it, to let the failures drag me down and keep me from doing better. I'd made sure I'd learned a lesson from each scar, and despite everything, I was doing well. I wasn't the scared kid everyone called gutter trash anymore. I was Sephyr Kasdaan, a merc and bounty hunter good enough to have caught the attention of Serr'eza and his th'rak brotherhood.

And the attention of a gorgeous human female. One that had the kind of stark, regal beauty of a queen but the soft curves of a bed companion. Our time together had been painfully brief, but she was clearly a bright and caring person. Her daughter had been a surprising contrast of wry humor and fierce protectiveness that reminded me of myself when I was younger. But it was Eva my mind kept latching onto, the way she'd taken me in, lingering on my broad shoulders and thick limbs, as if she liked what she was looking at and wanted to see more.

Suddenly my cock was twitching and filling against my leg, intense heat suffusing my belly. How long had it been since someone had looked at me like that? How long had it been since I *wanted* someone to look at me like that? My hand closed around my stiff length with a groan, imagining the spark in her gray eyes and how it might have flared if we'd been alone, if I was laying her down on my bed and stripping those clothes off of her body. I tried to imagine what color her nipples were, what her cunt might look like bare and dripping for me.

My hand was moving, pumping my length in a fist, my balls already tight and pulled up close to my body. I groaned, my head tilting back against the wall of the shower, my other hand sliding down to tug gently on my sac before sliding back up to swirl my fingertip around the rim of my sleeve, the shallow opening yvrenii males had just above their cocks to accommodate the female prod, ensuring they stayed locked together during sex (apparently, my ancestors on that side had had to try and procreate while running). But it was sensitive, especially around the rim, and I swirled my finger in time with my hand furiously pumping my shaft. In no time at all my muscles were tensing as my orgasm boiled down my spine, snapping it straight, and then my cock was bucking in my hand, thick hot ropes of my seed painting the shower floor. I sank my finger into my sleeve, feeling it clench and suck on the digit as my orgasm tore through me.

When it was finally over my legs were shivery and weak. Heart still hammering in my chest, I finished cleaning myself up and stepped out of the shower, drying off and getting dressed in the loose overlarge t-shirt I favored for bed. I disliked any kind of pants for sleeping; all they ever did was get tangled on my legs and tug painfully on the thicker fur of my lower half. I did have some basketball shorts I could wear if I had company overnight, but since it was just me I didn't bother.

When I checked my phone, a wide grin split my face, pulling my lips tight over my small tusks.

Eva: I like your enthusiasm. Me and Maggie go out for dinner every Sat. Does that work?

The idea of all three of us going out to dinner felt...good. Natural. Sure, I wouldn't be able to lay on my seductions too thick with a cub there, but the thought of getting to know both of them at once was...exciting.

The thought made me frown. Where were these feelings coming from? I'd never been the domestic type, but after one conversation with a human female I was suddenly picturing cozy nights in, my two females curled up in front of the television while I prepared them a meal. I was picturing going out to parks for walks and going to see the Bean and figuring out what its appeal was. It looked a little like a Billieuan transport shuttle tipped onto its front, and I was curious. It did strange things to my chest, to imagine celebrating the gift-giving holiday of Christmas with them, with Santa and Jesus and the elves delivering gifts to kind children and punishing those who had sinned. I'd seen several films about it recently, and wanted to try it very badly—and now when I pictured it, I saw Eva and Maggie in my living room beside a huge fir tree.

Me: I'd love to. Do you want to meet me at Leonie's or should I pick you up?

Eva: Let's meet. How's 5:30 so we miss the worst of the dinner rush?

Me: Sounds great.

We finished finalizing our plans, and just like that, I had a date. I didn't think I stopped smiling the entire night.

Chapter 5

Pizza Party

<u>EVA</u>

"Maybe I should just tell him to forget it," I sighed as yet another outfit failed to look good in the mirror. I shouldn't have been so concerned about whether or not what I wore would impress Seth. It wasn't like this was a serious date—I mean, for god's sake Maggie was coming with. But maybe because it had been so long since I'd been out on *any* date, even a casual one that was more like a hangout, I was twisting myself up over it and freaking out.

"You look great, Mom," Maggie assured me, wearing her usual black layers and heavy eyeliner. Today she'd also gone to the trouble of backcombing her hair and putting in her extensions, one of which was an adorable stripey thing done up in the trans flag colors—it was the only thing on her not stark black. I got a real kick out of seeing my daughter adopt the scene look I'd been too afraid to try back in high school. It looked good on her, and I liked that she was trying things to express herself. "Besides, you already made the brownies," she added. If Seth wasn't going to let me pay for dinner then I'd be damned if I wasn't going to at least cover dessert, but I'd made a huge batch to account for the appetites of two adults and a growing teen and locked myself into bringing them.

I fluffed the skirt of my dress, frowning at myself in the mirror. "I know I look alright, but we're just going for pizza. This feels too fancy." I bit my lip, then peered into my closet as if the perfect outfit would suddenly materialize and save me from myself.

"Then just wear jeans and a t-shirt. If he can't handle you at your casual pizza date then maybe he doesn't deserve you at your MET Gala red carpet look."

I laughed, shooting a look at her over my shoulder. "It's not *that* fancy, Mags." I bit my lip again, considering what she'd said. Maybe she had a point. I almost never dressed up in my free time, preferring comfort to looking "pretty" or "feminine" in the traditional sense. Besides, I'd still have makeup on and my hair done up—that was already finished. "You know what, you're right, baby. If he doesn't like my amazing t-shirts then he's not worth my time."

Maggie snorted, playing with her insanely long extensions. "Hell yeah, Moms. That's the spirit!" She ducked out of my bedroom so that I could change, and I slipped out of the nice cocktail dress I'd been wearing and into my favorite jeans and my latest shirt acquisition.

Some people collected shoes or jewelry or purses, but I was all about collecting shirts. I had to have at least fifty, and they ranged in absurdity from standard pop culture appreciation to obscure memes and my favorite fringe interests. It was hands down the dorkiest thing about me, and the more I thought about it the more right it felt that I dress like this tonight. I was thirty-five; I didn't have the time or energy to waste on something that wasn't going to go anywhere because of something as petty as clothing taste. And if he had expectations about how I was going to present myself then squashing those now was a great idea. It would hurt, of course, because *damn* was he cute, but it was smart, too.

"'Lasaga?'" Maggie kissed her pursed fingertips in a chef's kiss. "Perfection, Mother. If he doesn't propose by the end of the night he doesn't deserve you."

I threw my head back, laughing. "You're nuts, kid. But I think it's important to sus out whether or not a potential partner is going to have a compatible sense of humor. Or like your true self." Even if you could bounce a quarter off Seth's pert round butt and that grin of his could melt panties, it wouldn't be worth my time to get involved with him if he thought the things I liked were dumb, or if he didn't want anything to do with my daughter after spending more time with her—which was why I hadn't fought her coming along.

Me and Maggie piled into my trusty silver Corolla and started heading to the restaurant. I could see out of the corner of my eye that Maggie was on her phone, scrolling through one of her social media feeds. "You're sure you're okay with this?" I asked her, chewing my lip. "It's okay if you're not, honey. I haven't dated anyone since you've been alive and I'd totally understand if you didn't—"

"*Mom*," Maggie groaned, dropping her phone into her lap. "I'm fourteen, I can handle the idea of my mom dating. Hell, I *want* you to date. You deserve to be with someone and—um, you just do."

I narrowed my eyes at the road, since I couldn't glare directly at her. "What were you going to say there?" I asked warily. That had definitely sounded like she'd cut herself off.

"Nothing!"

"Mags."

"It's nothing! Just...I don't know, sometimes I feel bad, I guess. That you make yourself lonely and miserable for me."

She could have spit in my face and shocked me less. "You think I'm miserable?"

"Well, you're not *happy*. You're having panic attacks so *something* is fucked." Her voice got softer, tighter, and her speech sped up rapidly, so that she was practically spitting her words out, "And the fact that you haven't even gone on a date at all since you had me makes me think it's my fault. Like you can't be happy because of me."

My eyes got hot, and I had to blink rapidly to be able to keep a clear view of the road. So much for my mascara. "Honey," I said in a rasp, shooting a glance at her. "That isn't true at all. I want you to listen to me: you are *the best thing* to ever happen to me. *Ever*. Do you understand? If I haven't dated it's been *my* choice, and it's because I love you so much that I want to make sure your life is as perfect as I can make it, and dating wouldn't have helped any of that." I pursed my lips, trying to stop the wobble that was threatening to steal my words. "Dating just wasn't worth the distraction to me, alright? You didn't stop me from doing *anything*."

"If you say so," she said, picking her phone back up. "Seth seems pretty nice, so I'm glad you're letting yourself do this." I could tell she didn't want to talk about it anymore, so I let it drop; we were almost at the restaurant, anyway.

When we pulled into the lot it was almost completely filled, and I let out a sigh as I resigned myself to driving around in circles for way too long trying to find a spot. So much for missing the dinner rush.

It was ten minutes before I managed to snag something, and the two of us were officially late for my date, but I'd had

Mags text him from my phone when the first sweep of the lot had yielded nothing.

He was waiting for us by the front door, dressed in all black and looking sexy as sin. His huge arms were crossed over his chest, making his pecs and biceps bulge. He wasn't slim by any means, which had always been my preference, and all of that delicious bulk on display was making it a little hard to breathe. Not to mention how much more of his tattoos I could see now that he was wearing a t-shirt instead of a henley—they were abstract designs, swooping lines and geometric shapes that were beautiful despite how simple they were.

"There you are. Glad you finally found parking," he called, pushing off the wall with a grin. "I put in our names for a table but they haven't summoned me yet." He waved a black puck in the air I hadn't spotted before, which I recognized as the pagers that the restaurant used.

"Oh, that's good. Thank you for that," I managed, my eyes aching with the urge to keep checking him out. His curly mop of ginger hair was tousled in a way that was so perfect it had to be intentional, and I found that I suddenly couldn't think of a single thing to say to him. You could have held a gun to my head and I wouldn't have been able to come up with a single thing a human asked another human to get to know them on a date.

Luckily Seth wasn't so tongue-tied. "I like your shirt," he said to me, nodding at me with his chin. "I love Garfield memes. Bold of you to wear it tonight. I assume you thought I'd be impressed by your appreciation of a fellow ginger?"

I laughed, surprised that he got the niche meta-meme emblazoned on my torso. "It was actually a test to tell me whether or not you have good taste."

Seth turned to Maggie and stage whispered, "You think I passed?"

"Oh yeah," she confirmed. "I don't even fully get that one so you like, probably outrank me now."

Seth laughed, his gorgeous golden eyes crinkling, and I thought I might kiss him just for that, for being so...open with my daughter, for so easily keeping her included.

The little puck buzzed and flashed in Seth's huge hand, startling us, and we moved inside to answer the summons and claim our table.

We were seated at an actual table rather than a booth, and I found myself hesitating about where I should sit. I didn't want Maggie to have to sit next to Seth when she didn't know him very well, but on dates I was pretty sure you usually sat across from your date so you didn't crowd each other and could see each other clearly. *Fuck it,* I thought, settling into the seat next to him so Maggie could sit on my other side. I was still on a different side of the little square table from him, so I'd still be able to see him well enough for conversation.

Also, I was probably overthinking this. Like, by a lot. But social situations had always been a kind of minefield for me, and when I actually cared about them going right it shot my anxiety right off the charts. If I was lucky, *all* I'd do was overthink.

Seth shot me a smirk as I sat down, his canines looking unusually sharp now that I was a little closer. But more important than that was the fact that this man smelled fucking *amazing*. I'd never in my life experienced such an immediate attraction to how someone smelled, and it seized me so fast and so hard that I got a little dizzy. *What on earth is that cologne?* I tried to lean in and sniff him more deeply without being a creep about it. He smelled so good I was practically drooling.

Our server plopped a couple of menus on the table and promised to be right back for our drink orders, and then it was just the three of us.

Seth scooped up one of the menus and flipped through it briefly. "I've never been here before, so maybe I'll let you two lead and tell me what's good."

"I only eat two things," Maggie drawled, slumped into her seat and playing with the ends of her extensions. "Sausage pizza and mozzarella sticks."

"No veggies, huh?" Seth asked.

"It's the texture of the vegetables," I explained, wanting to defend my daughter's pickiness. "The texture that they get when you bake them grosses her out. Except for olives. But they gross *me* out so we usually just get plain sausage."

Seth smiled, nodding. "I can see that. I get something like that with certain fruits and veggies when they're raw. Like raw celery? I think I might prefer crunching into a bug."

I squealed and gently slapped at his thick bicep.

"You do not!"

"What? Lots of people eat insects. It's good protein. Cheap."

I giggled, pulling a face. "I was talking about your weird feelings about celery, but it's good to know you're pro-insect eating."

"Hey, don't knock it 'til you try it, Eva."

"Fair," I allowed, failing to suppress a smirk.

"Yeah Mom, stop being such a prude," Maggie chimed in, and I pretended to glare at her.

"*Et tu*, Mags?" I asked her, clutching at my heart. "If you two are going to gang up on me like this all the time I'm going to have to adopt another child just to make it even."

Maggie snorted, playing with a napkin by rolling it up as tight as she could.

"Well, I hate to keep being controversial when I'm trying so hard to make you like me," Seth said, making my eyes swing back to his intimidatingly handsome face, "but would you be offended if I got a little Hawaiian pizza?"

"Oh my god, Mom, you *have* to marry him," Maggie gasped, covering her mouth with her long pale hands. "He thinks your shirt's funny *and* he freakishly likes Hawaiian pizza, too? You're like, made for each other."

Seth laughed at her joke while I tried to get my burning face under control. Teenagers had the subtlety of a goddamn fire alarm. I didn't know much about modern dating but I *did* know that most men didn't appreciate marriage talk on the first date. "We just met, Maggie," I muttered, shooting Seth an apologetic look. But he didn't look uncomfortable; in fact, he was looking at me thoughtfully, like hearing marriage talk on the first date—which included the date's daughter, no less—wasn't making him want to run for the hills. *Maybe he's recently sustained head trauma. Or he comes from another planet where monogamous commitment is natural.*

"You thinking you'd rather not marry me, then?" Seth asked softly, leaning closer, gold eyes burning into mine. I swallowed, my throat so dry it clicked.

"I didn't say that," I heard myself murmur back. "Most guys would freak out hearing something like that so soon, though."

Seth shrugged, the piercings in his ears catching the light.

"Guess I'm not most guys, then. I know that I want something serious, and so far I really like you."

Was it hot in here or was it just me? It was like someone had been collecting all of my wildest relationship fantasies and had manufactured someone who hit all my buttons. If he also ate pussy like a fiend and thought staying in on Fridays was the height of luxury then maybe I *did* have to marry him.

I couldn't think of anything fun or flirty to say to that. All that popped out of my mouth was, "So how old are you, then?" My *foot is finding its way into my mouth a lot, lately.*

Seth hunched forward, resting his folded arms on the table. "Twenty-eight. Do you consider it rude if I ask how old you are?"

Ah, *there* was the catch. "I might be too old for you," I chuckled, my heart sinking. "I'm thirty-five."

He scoffed and waved his hand. "That's nothing. What is that, six years? Seven?"

I was *this* close to asking him if he was trying to scam me. Young, hot, unafraid of commitment, and cool with kids? Something didn't add up.

Just then our server returned, looking flustered and apologizing for the wait. Seth gave her one of his panty-melting grins and told her not to worry. She flushed but smiled gratefully, taking our drink orders and promising to be back in a second for our dinner order.

"You want to split a medium Hawaiian then and Maggie can get whatever her little heart desires all to herself?" Seth asked, taking a sip of his cola.

"Hell yes! I'm *definitely* getting black olives with the sausage," Maggie answered, doing a goofy little victory dance in her seat.

Seth laughed, cocking an eyebrow at her. "I still can't believe *that's* the vegetable you like on pizza."

Maggie threw her rolled-up napkin at his face. "Shut up, Seth. You like Hawaiian pizza, you don't get to talk shit about my olives." That just made him laugh harder, tossing the rolled-up napkin back to her side of the table.

"Fair," he chuckled, grabbing a napkin from the dispenser and folding it into an intricate shape that had me mesmerized. It kind of reminded me of origami, or of his tattoos. "It's not fair for me to discriminate against you just for liking one of the nastiest, saltiest little boogers—"

Maggie squealed at him, laughing, and my heart melted at the sight of them. It was so hard for my baby to be at ease like this with new people, but here was Seth making her relax and joke around like they'd been pals for years.

Marriage was looking more likely by the second.

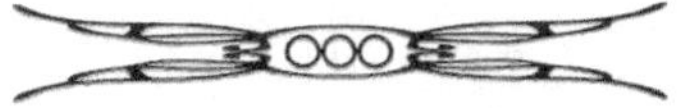

SEPHYR

I was pretty sure the date was going well, but I'd never been so nervous and sweaty before in my life.

Wanting a human female I could hide behind when I cut and run didn't quite explain the warm light that filled my chest when I made closed-off and quiet Maggie laugh at one of my silly jokes, or when I saw Eva glance at me with barely concealed desire. They actually *liked* me, and that was territory I'd never wound up in without more work than it was worth. It was hard keeping up that extra-shiny version of myself that people tended to find most palatable, so when I'd let it drop and they'd drop me it just kind of made sense. But there was something about Eva that made me feel like it was okay for me to be more relaxed, more like myself.

When the server next came around she dropped off a fresh cola for me and took our food order, promising it should only be a little while before we saw it. Once she'd left I turned to Eva and swirled my straw through my soda nervously.

"So, you want to just go ahead and get the standard boring first date stuff out of the way?" I asked her. I pointed at myself and listed off the basics—which I'd modified to their Earth equivalents but kept as close to the truth as possible; it made shit easier to remember when it was mostly true. "Parents died when I was a kid, no siblings. Grew up in the system and had kind of a rough start in life. Now I freelance, mostly in security and information."

Eva arched an eyebrow at me, giving me a look I couldn't quite read. She almost looked...disappointed? "You think getting to know someone is boring?" she asked, crossing her arms over her chest. *Vrakaash*, I'd fucked this up.

"Not at all," I rushed to reassure her, "But those are the questions that everyone asks just to ask them, you know? Because it's considered rude to ask the questions we really want the answers to on the first date."

Eva pressed her lips into a line and seemed to think about what I'd said. "And what are the questions you really want to know the answers to about me?" she asked softly, her eyes going shuttered.

I licked my lips, thinking. If I was dating this gorgeous woman for real, what would I want to know about her? "What do you dream about? What makes you laugh? Like *really* laugh, where you think you might pee yourself and you sound like you're dying." I kept thinking, my heart pounding in my chest and feeling raw. "Does it scare you that I'm this serious right away? Do you even want that?" I bit my lip, my armpits slippery with nervous sweat. "My life so far has been…troubled. Do you judge me for having a lot of bones in my closet?" Shit, was that the phrase? And why the hell was I still talking? But I couldn't seem to stop myself.

Finally, my mouth quit running away from itself, and I watched Eva's face carefully, her thick dark brows lowered in consideration.

She dropped her arms, folding her hands in her lap. "Thank you for being honest." She met my eyes, and there was something in their stormy depths that made me tingle. "And while I can't say I'm totally comfortable with the idea of dating someone with a record, I also believe that people can change. And a lot of crime happens because people don't get taken care of right and are forced to make some hard, desperate choices. It's more important to me that you seem like a nice guy *now*. A degenerate wouldn't stop to help a stranger having a panic attack by the frozen pizza and agree to a group date with said stranger's teenage daughter.

"As for that other stuff…" she hesitated, peeking at me from under her eyelashes. "Commitment doesn't scare me. But I hope you understand that because I have Maggie, I'm not going to just jump into something." I nodded, and she cleared her throat. "And I guess I dream about being able to open my own bakery. It's just a hobby but baking is my happy place. My job is alright, it pays the bills," a strange look crossed her face, there and gone in a second, "it doesn't also have to be fulfilling. And…Maggie makes me laugh. And goofy shit that I see on the internet. People can be so creative and funny."

I couldn't seem to stop smiling at her, this gorgeous and surprising female. "I appreciate that you're willing to give me a chance," I told her, surprised by my earnestness. "Though it's kind of sad that you feel like you can't follow your dreams. What's stopping you?"

She shrugged. "It's just too expensive, too risky. Maybe down the line, or if the economy magically improves, but for now, it's enough that I get to do it in my free time."

I frowned, but it wasn't like I was a stranger to being in that position. Hell, I was in that position *now*—taking a gig just because it got me where I needed to go, even though it was so awful I'd rather chew my own leg off than go through with it. "We'll get you there," I heard myself say, startling me. A male with a bounty on his head wasn't going to be in any position to make dreams come true. I mentally shook myself and smiled at her again. "Is there anything else you're curious about with me?"

She bit her pretty pink lip, clearly warring with herself. I braced for whatever it was she was going to ask. "I guess I'm still stuck wondering why you wanted this so bad. I'm more than half a decade older than you and I have a kid. I was a mess when we first met. I'm not the best and figuring out when something is strange but...I guess I'm just stuck wondering."

I swallowed, considering what to tell her. "Well, I guess it's just like I said before: I really like you, and I'm looking for something more serious, more long-term. And I figured why not get to know you and your daughter more at the same time? You're a package deal, so if she doesn't like me now would be a good time to find that out." I glanced at Maggie with a smile that felt unusually shy. "Right, kid? What's my score looking like so far?"

Maggie shrugged, typing away at her phone and flushing a little. "You get points for having cool tattoos and for being nice to my mom, but you've got a lot of ground to make up for the pizza."

I laughed, something like relief making me feel light. "Well, you forgave your mom for it so there's hope. I'll take it." I returned my attention to Eva, going tense again. "Does that answer your question? Or do you want to know more?"

She bit her lip, her eyes searching my face. "It does answer my question," she hedged, tucking a tendril of her dark hair behind her ear, "but it might take a while for me to believe it. I hope it doesn't offend you if it sounds too good to be true."

I nodded, swirling my straw in my half-empty glass of cola. "No, I get it. This means I just gotta make sure I don't blow my chance to show you I mean it." I held her gaze when she looked at me, hoping that I looked trustworthy and earnest enough. There was something inside me that *needed* her to believe me, something that went deeper than wanting to get away from Serr'eza, deeper than the part of me left over from my lonely childhood that wanted people to like me. There was something about *her*, about Eva, that called to me and made me want to get closer.

Our food arrived then, easing the subtle tension that had built up.

"This is really good," I said appreciatively. "Best I've had yet."

"Mom used to work here," Maggie told me around a half-chewed mouthful of food.

Eva flushed, swatting at her daughter. "Like a decade ago! I have nothing to do with how the pizza tastes *now*, goof."

I smiled at her, taking another sip of my cola. "So modest. I bet if we went back to the kitchen they'd have a shrine to you back there. You give off that vibe."

She laughed. "What on earth does *that* mean?"

I shrugged. "You seem like the sort of person who changes people's lives regularly and is completely unaware of it."

"That's a type of person?"

Mouth full, I nodded emphatically.

"Well, I hate to break it to you, because you seem like the type who hates to be wrong—" I grunted indignantly, but had to fight back a smile. There may have been some truth to that. "But I can assure you I've never had that kind of an impact on a person's life. I work from home for a call center. I didn't even finish college, I only got an associate's."

I frowned at her, wiping grease from my face with one of the paper napkins. "What, so you have to have a fancy degree to make a difference? Some of the best people I've ever known have been 'low-class' and 'uneducated'." I turned to Maggie. "Back me up, Mags. Your mom is a saint who is completely clueless about her charms."

Maggie grinned. "Oh, yeah. She gets our elderly neighbor's groceries for her and *never* tells her the full amount it costs because she knows she's on a fixed income. She gives service workers snacks and never *ever* yells at them no matter how rude or slow they're being. And, and, *and* she bakes a cake for literally everyone's birthday and never takes money for it."

Eva sputtered, red creeping up her throat. "Those are just things people do for each other! It's nothing special."

I *tsked*. "See? Clueless." Maggie giggled while Eva glared at me. But it was a venomless glare. I thought she might have even secretly liked it. She probably did all this nice stuff for the people around her and never got recognition for it. She clearly wasn't doing it so people would worship her, but who didn't like their efforts being appreciated?

Maybe that was why Eva was having panic attacks: she gave everything of herself to others, and had neglected herself for so long that her brain was forcing her to pay attention in the only way she'd notice.

For some reason, that made me really mad. What the fuck were the people in Eva's life doing, that they were letting her just run herself ragged like that? *I can take care of her. I'd take* good *care of her. She's a fine woman and deserves to be treated like a treasure,* I found myself thinking. Well, that didn't matter. I wasn't going to be able to be that for her, no matter how much I wanted it.

I took another bite of pizza, but all the pleasure I'd felt for its taste had disappeared, my food turning to lead in my stomach.

Fuck it: maybe I couldn't be that male for her in the long term, but I could give her that treatment while I was around. Show her a good time, make her feel good. And then when I had to leave it would hurt, but at least I could rest easier knowing I'd given Eva my best. That I'd done everything I could to make her life easier while I was with her.

I wiped the grease off my fingers and grabbed the hand she was resting on the table. "I know it's still early in the date, but I gotta ask: when can I see you again?"

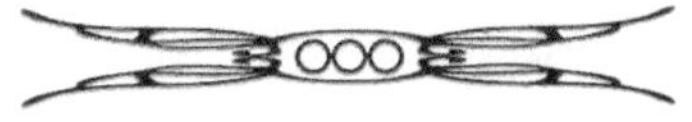

EVA

Maggie, no doubt thinking she was being very helpful, interjected: "She's not doing anything tomorrow. You could go out for lunch or some shit, just the two of you."

I sighed and looked at my daughter. "Magdalena, you are not my pimp. Please let me do this myself."

She snorted, leveling an *are you serious?* look at me. "If I don't push you, you're not going to let yourself go for it. You never do. So now you have to deal with me taking charge."

My instinct was to get mad, to do what my mother would have done and "put my foot down" by pulling rank and belittling her input. But I was trying to break the generational trauma, to end the granite lineage I'd come from and raise my child with warmth and understanding, so I took a few slow breaths and gathered myself. "I appreciate that you're concerned for me, honey. That you want me to pursue more things. But I am an adult and I need to be able to handle this myself."

Seth watched us closely, looking surprised. I felt my face flame, but if he thought us strange I wouldn't let that come between me and raising my child. "I gotta learn how to do it myself, right?"

Maggie nodded, taking another bite of her pizza. "Fair. I will take off my feathered purple pimp hat and put on my coach hat and binoculars." She mimed swapping headgear with a flourish that had me and Seth both chuckling. I was still feeling a little angry, but I felt like that moment had gone fairly well.

"I've never seen that before," Seth said slowly. "That...whatever that was. That kind of exchange. It was remarkable."

I shrugged, my face still hot and no doubt beet red. "It's

uh, called gentle parenting. My parents were really strict with me and I vowed I wouldn't hurt my child like that, so when I was pregnant with Maggie I did a lot of research."

Seth smiled, looking between us with interest. "Fascinating. I like it. The more I find out about you the more I find to like, Eva." If I blushed any harder I was going to wind up fainting.

"It's just treating kids like the tiny humans they are. I didn't come up with it or anything." But I was preening just a little bit at the praise. It was hard doing things this way, but it *was* worth it. "But she *is* right, we could do lunch tomorrow if you're available. I know Sunday isn't the hottest date day but you've already survived pizza dinner with my teenage daughter so why not, right?"

Seth grinned at me, dabbing at his full lips with a napkin. "That sounds perfect. I'll have to come up with something to knock your socks off in a hurry, but I like a challenge."

Maggie pushed away from the table with a loud sigh. "Man, I sure do have to go to the bathroom," she announced, throwing me a broad wink. "I'll probably be in there for at least fifteen minutes."

I laughed, rolling my eyes at my daughter's antics. "Okay, have a nice time. I promise I won't leave without you!"

She glared at me, stuffing her phone in her back pocket. "You better not; if I die here I swear I am going to haunt you *so bad*." Then she was heading for the bathroom doors at the back of the restaurant.

"I like her spirit," Seth chuckled, turning to me. "You're really letting her be herself." He sat back, tossing his used napkins onto his empty plate to show he was done.

I smiled at him, fidgeting a little in my chair. Now that it was just the two of us and I was getting his full attention, it was almost too much. His golden eyes were trained on mine with laser focus, like I was the only woman on Earth, and while I liked it I couldn't help also finding it uncomfortable in its intensity. I'd never been a great beauty, and between my mom bod and having hidradenitis supporitiva, things hadn't exactly improved. I knew I wasn't much of a catch. But Seth was looking at me like I was.

"Are you alright, Eva?" he asked me softly, his hand sliding towards me on the table, "Have I said something to upset you?"

Jesus, what was I *doing*? Here was this sweet guy who was totally into me, good with my daughter, and I was just sitting there letting myself freak out about things that hadn't even happened yet. I reached out and took his hand, not letting myself hesitate. He smiled at me, his curiously pointed canines glittering in the low lighting. Then he flipped his hand under mine and threaded our fingers together. Tingling electricity shot down my spine at the contact, at how delicious his warm, rough palm felt against mine. I couldn't seem to stop myself from imagining what those hands would feel like on other parts of my body.

"I'm sorry I'm being so weird," I told him, pressing my lips into a line and squirming in my seat as heat pooled low in my belly. "I'm really...rusty. Haven't really dated since I got pregnant with Maggie. But I'm glad we met."

"I'm really glad, too," Seth said, scooting his chair a little closer to mine. "I don't mind a little bit of rust. You wear it well." He squeezed my hand, leaning closer, until it felt like my whole world had shrunk to just Seth, his woodsmoke and spice scent making me thrum, his gold eyes pulling me in like a riptide. "I don't know how many times I'm going to have to say this, but I'll keep saying it until you believe me: I *like* you. I want to get to know you. So if the feeling's still mutual then I'm going to have to put my foot down and tell you you can't talk about yourself like that the rest of the night."

Oh fuck, that is so hot, I thought, having to dig my nails into my thigh under the table to stop myself from whimpering. Since when did I think bossy guys were sexy? But there was something about this that was 100% doing it for me. It wasn't like, "I know best so do what I tell you," it was like, "you need someone to take care of you and I'm going to do it" bossy and that made all the difference.

"Yes, sir," I managed in a husky whisper.

For some reason, that was when I remembered the brownies. I gently tugged my hand free, reaching behind me to dig around in my purse, hanging off the back of my chair to rest near my side. I pulled out the saran-wrapped parcel, sliding it to him across the table like we were commencing a drug deal. "I-I didn't want to forget but I made these. For you."

He took the parcel, turning it over in his hands and peering at it curiously. "What is it?"

"Brownies. I crumbled Oreo's on the top so they're *very* rich."

"And you made these just for me?"

I shrugged, uncomfortable with how…overwhelmed he looked. "Well, I made a little extra so Maggie wouldn't murder me in my sleep for not letting her have some."

He bit his lip, the stud under the middle of his bottom lip twinkling in the low light. "Thank you so much for this. It…it means a lot."

I chuckled. "It's just brownies. To thank you for being so nice."

He leaned close, pecking a kiss to my cheek. It was quick, the very image of chaste, but my body reacted like he'd done so much more, my nipples prickling to attention and goosebumps breaking out all over my body. I was breathless from that brief contact, my whole world fading away to copper hair and golden eyes. "Nothing 'just' about it, gorgeous," he murmured, his pupils expanding.

"Now who's the one who doesn't know how to see their worth?" I murmured, cocking an eyebrow at him. He started like I'd hit him, his lips gently parted as he stared at me. Then a smile spread slow and sweet on his face.

"Alright then, Miss Eva. I see how it is." He lifted the bundle and nodded at me. "But thank you for these."

My skin tingled and shivered, heat like I'd never known washing through me. I was lost in his face, in his scent, aching for him like I'd never done before for anyone else.

We spotted Maggie emerging from the bathroom and shifted further apart, giving me a chance to breathe and compose myself before she slouched back into her seat, eyeing our clasped hands with a smirk.

Despite our meal being finished we lingered—something I basically never did, especially on a busy night, knowing they needed our table—but I just couldn't manage to tear myself away from Seth. He kept hold of my hand until I had to excuse myself for the restroom, and then once I was back he picked it right back up like he couldn't stand not touching me, trailing his thumb over my skin, as he finished up telling Maggie about the meaning behind one of his tattoos.

God, he was so good with her. Kind but still teasing and

fun. I liked that he treated her like she was a buddy without getting overly familiar or pushing her boundaries. A lot of my friends didn't even do that, giving her hugs and touching her without asking first—which had led to more than one fight when my friends insisted they weren't doing anything wrong.

When it was finally time to head home, walking away from him after just a too-brief hug was one of the hardest things I'd ever done. I felt like I was gliding, slipping and sliding through the rest of my evening like I was high, my thoughts snagged thoroughly on Seth.

Chapter 6

Tectonic Shifts

<u>SEPHYR</u>

When I finally managed to pull myself away from Eva and her firecracker of a kid it was later than I'd planned on getting back to my place, and I groaned when I saw a missed comm from Serr'eza, followed by a textcom asking for an update. It was clear that the th'rakk wasn't in the mood to wait, so I fired up the signal relay and returned his call. One of Serr'eza's most infuriating traits was his unwillingness to use text-based communications; he was old-fashioned and thought business was best done face-to-face or, at the very least, voice-to-voice.

"Where were you this evening?" Serr'eza snapped as soon as the connection stabilized. "I've been trying for hours."

I bit back a sigh. "Touring potential properties for the front organization."

Despite his lack of a face in the conventional sense, I had the feeling Serr'eza was frowning at me. "What is taking so long, Kasdaan? Why have you not already secured the property?"

"There's a lot of regulations and requirements for opening an orphanage. It's been difficult finding something that will allow me to pass inspections and get properly certified. If this place is even a little suspicious we'll draw unwanted attention from the local authorities."

"I don't give a whiff of *vrakaash* about the human authorities. I need *merchandise*, you pathetic mutt."

I sucked in a breath, letting myself curl my lip at Serr'eza's holographic image. "Fuck you, th'rak. You want this done fast then get the first asshole you come across with a stiffy for proving himself. But if you want a solid front that can bring in a steady stream of merchandise for you and your customers —"

"Fine!" Serr'eza snarled, his biolights flaring all at once. His eyes narrowed. "Check back in in one week. If you still haven't made progress I'm sending in Siit'ron to remind you of who's working for whom, here."

A spark of fear arced through me, but I managed to keep my face expressionless. "There's Collective enforcers in orbit right now. They've been here the whole time I have." It wasn't a lie, either; I regularly checked my camera feeds and scanned the skies for their craft, and they hadn't budged yet. I was starting to worry they'd detected me here after all.

"I have ways of getting my people where I need them." Serr'eza promised in a low growl. "You give me a concrete update by this time next week, or Siit'ron uses his considerable talents to flay you alive. Am I understood?"

"Yes," I growled, wishing I could rip him to shreds with my claws.

"Good."

The connection cut out, leaving me staring at a blank wall. I cursed, tearing off my wristcom and tossing it on a nearby table. I'd have to move my timeline up considerably now that

Serr'eza was getting impatient, which meant I'd be busy as hell this next week. I considered canceling with Eva to be able to focus more fully on my escape, but as soon as the thought crossed my mind I felt sick. Sure, I didn't want to have to tangle with Serr'eza's most bloodthirsty lieutenant, but I'd been planning this for a while; surely I could bring everything together and manage to see the gorgeous human female I'd gotten myself so smitten with?

I sighed, turning towards my bedroom so I could strip and get ready for bed. It was late, and I was too tired to figure it all out now.

Once my teeth were brushed and my face washed I stripped down to my briefs and slid into bed.

"Sleep mode," I barked, and the lights immediately shut off and soft night sounds started playing from a concealed speaker. I grabbed my eyemask from the nightstand and slipped it on, laying on my back and folding my hands over my stomach.

I tried to clear my mind, to shut my dumb brain off so I could get some sleep and put that nasty conversation with Serr'eza behind me, but it seemed like the harder I tried the more it slipped away.

I tore off my mask with a growl and snatched my phone from the nightstand where it was charging. At first, using something so physical had bothered me, feeling strange after a lifetime of using holoscreens, but I had to admit it had grown on me. There was something nice about the tactility of having to touch a piece of glass. I unlocked the screen and stared at the home screen, not sure what to do to distract myself.

I clicked on my messaging app idly, scrolling through the

brief conversation thread between me and Eva. I smiled, thinking about how pink she'd gotten when she'd been embarrassed, how she was a curious blend of snarky and sweet that had me dying to know more about her. How else was she a dichotomy? What would she be like first thing in the morning? How did she like to sleep at night? Would she find my noise machine and sleep mask ridiculous?

I wondered what she would think of my past, if she ever got to know it in more detail—but no, she never would. She'd have to know I wasn't from Earth for that. But I couldn't seem to stop myself from wondering...and in the wondering I found myself yearning, aching for the intimacy of someone knowing so much about me, seeing all the dark and dirty corners of my soul, and deciding to love me anyway.

Not that Eva would necessarily *love* me. No one had before, and I wasn't going to be able to be honest enough with her to encourage love now. That was just part of the fantasy.

I started typing out a new message to Eva, telling myself I'd just check in on her and then I'd try to sleep again.

Me: Hey you. just wanted to say I had a lot of fun tonight, and I can't wait to see you tomorrow.

When the message switched to "read" and the three thinking dots sprang up pretty much right away something strange happened to my chest. My heart felt like it was grinding to a halt and speeding up faster than it should have all at the same time, and I couldn't stop the grin that spread across my face.

Eva: Hey yourself. I had a good time too. Will you hate me if I say I was surprised that I had as much fun as I did?

I laughed, grinning at the little glowing screen.

Me: I'd expect nothing less from you. In your defense, I could have been a real creep. Some sicko who gets off on helping strangers get through panic attacks.

She sent a gif of a person looking shocked.

Eva: You make it seem like I'm crazy to be cautious. When you get to be my age you learn that sometimes you DO need to look a gift horse in the mouth.

I looked up that strange phrase, assuming it was some sort of English idiom. "To look in a critical way at something..." Ah.

Me: You think I'm a gift, gorgeous? Well, I HAVE been told that I'm basically god's gift to women...

She sent me another moving picture, this one of someone saying "no" a whole bunch of times. I'd have to get her to tell me how she was doing that so quickly.

Eva: I cannot believe you. The AUDACITY of this man!!! After a moment she started typing again. *I wouldn't go so far as to say you're a gift...but I DO like you. You're not what I expected and I like that.*
Me: what were you expecting?
Eva: A douchebag who uses women to get what he wants. But

there's way easier and prettier pickins than me so if all you wanted was an easy meal you'd never waste your time on me.

I sent her several stern frowny face emojis.

Me: How dare you insult the woman I'm courting! I'll have to fight you for her honor
Eva: COURTING?! Omg are you SURE you're 28??
Me: Don't change the subject, ma'am. This is very serious. I'm well within my rights to demand satisfaction. I will accept a kiss on the cheek of your choosing as recompense for besmirching m'lady's honor.
Eva: I...seriously don't know what to make of that. Are you like, secretly a huge Jane Austen fan or something?

I chuckled, grinning wider at the screen.

Me: Charlotte Bronte, actually. Stop changing the subject. Eva Nadzija is beautiful, kind, intelligent, giving, and hilarious and I won't let anyone say anything to the contrary.

I threw in another couple of frowny faces to make sure she got the message.

The three dots stayed on the screen for a long time, and my heart sank thinking I'd genuinely upset her.

Eva: You really think that about me?

she asked at last, and it felt like something in me cracked. I could practically hear her asking me that in a tiny, scared little voice.

Me: Of course. I'm many things but I'm not a flatterer. And I don't waste my time on people who I don't like.

My short tail started wriggling under me in irritation. For some reason, it was really important to me that she believed me. That she understood just how wonderful she was. How much...how much I wished I could pursue her for real, and not just because it would ease my escape.

Me: You're a catch. And I'm lucky to have met you, I added before I could second guess it.

Eva: I'm starting to think I'm pretty lucky to have met you too, Seth, she responded after a while, making my heart do that strange thing in my chest again. Was I coming down with something? It was very strange but somehow pleasant, and I both did and did not want it to keep happening.

We continued talking like that late into the night, well past the point where I was tired enough to sleep, talking about whatever we could. Despite Eva being older than me and a parent, she had a goofy side to her that was a joy to tease out —and the later it got the goofier she became, until I was lying in bed crying with laughter at the things she was saying.

It had been a long time since I'd felt this free talking to someone. Hell, it had been a long-ass time since I'd talked this much to a person, period.

Brunch couldn't come soon enough.

Chapter 7

Take Her to Brunch, First

<u>EVA</u>

Last night had been one of the weirdest first dates I'd ever been on, but it might have also been one of the best. I was tingling and fluttering for hours afterward, giggling like a kid over the texts he sent me way too late into the night. And even once I silenced my phone and went to bed I couldn't sleep; images of the way his shoulders and arms had flexed under that tight black shirt, the way his golden eyes had crinkled when he blasted me with one of those delicious grins, had had me so worked up I'd had no choice but to break out my vibrator and ride it until I was too sensitive and exhausted to keep going.

I should have been worn out and cranky this morning, but somehow the spell Seth had wrought with his gentle teasing and surprising honesty was still in full effect. Maybe it had something to do with the text I'd woken up to after a very disappointing four hours of sleep:

Seth: Good morning, gorgeous. I'm sure you'll be pleased to know I barely slept all night thinking about you.

* * *

I'd bitten my lip, smiling like a crazy person as I'd thought back to my own sleepless night.

Me: Good morning yourself, handsome. Can't say I slept well either. Good thing it's Sunday I guess, huh?

Seth: Spoken like a true 9-5er. Some of us have to work every day of the week.

Then he sent a gif of someone crossing their arms and looking judgmental. He'd been curious how I sent gifs, so I'd shown him last night, and he was going nuts sending me all kinds of weird things, just because he could.

I'd created a monster.

I let myself lie in bed chatting for another fifteen minutes, then hauled myself up to start my day. Maggie was still asleep and probably would be for a while, so I brushed my teeth and hopped in the shower. It had been a long time since I'd woken up in such a good mood—a fact which was especially shocking because of my lack of sleep—and I knew it was absolutely Seth's fault. It made me feel a little guilty though, realizing that it took doing something selfish to feel this good. Why couldn't I manage this amount of joy and enthusiasm for the important things in life, like raising my daughter and earning a living?

I shook my head, wondering if those thoughts weren't maybe a little unhealthy. Just because I wasn't always *giddy* about doing things for Maggie, that didn't mean I didn't still find joy and satisfaction in it.

Shit, no wonder I was so stressed all the time. I sighed, getting dressed in clean pajamas (since I'd have to change for my date anyway) and clapped my hands in excitement; before my brunch date with Seth I had another date with some dough. I wasn't about to let this precious free time slip by me. I *lived* for the weekends, when I could spend real time with Maggie and indulge in my passion for baking.

I'd been waiting all week to conquer my fear of sourdough and get a starter going. Maggie had finished her huge jar of pickle spears last weekend and I'd saved the jar just for this. It had been hours of reading blogs, comparing recipes, and watching videos just to be sure I had it, but I finally felt ready.

I washed and dried my jar again just to be totally certain it wasn't contaminated, then broke out my food scale and measured out my flour and my water and whisked it with a fork until it was smooth and fully blended. Then, according to all my research, all that was left to do was cover it and let it sit. I'd have to feed it after a certain point and watch it closely for signs of it going bad, but by all accounts, I'd been successful so far.

That done, I moved on to the banana bread I'd been saving my brown bananas for. I popped in my earbuds and put on my favorite playlist of hits from my teenhood.

When Maggie finally hauled herself out of bed, it was to find me shaking my butt and carefully pouring banana bread batter into greased pans while I sang along to classic Xtina. I saw her laugh, clapping her hands and doing a little dance of her own. When I popped out my earbuds she was singing a goofy song about how she was excited about banana bread to the tune of "Fighter", which was what I had been listening to.

I laughed with her, pecking a kiss on her cheek as I passed her to deposit my goodies into the oven. "'Morning, sweetie," I greeted.

"You're in a *very* good mood today," she told me, her voice still thick with sleep. "I take it that has something to do with a certain redheaded man?"

I shrugged, my face heating. "Maaaaybe. Maybe I'm just really excited about this banana bread. And the sourdough starter I finally got around to." She wrinkled her nose, eyeing the covered jar sitting on the counter skeptically. "Or…" I bit my lip, considering. "Maybe I *am* excited to see Seth again. But in a very cool, adult way that makes you respect me."

Maggie snorted, folding her arms over her chest. "Don't tell Mom this, but I actually respect her plenty," she told me, her cheeks flushing pink and her toes wriggling in discomfort. "And I'm glad she's excited and having fun."

I swallowed around the lump in my throat. "My lips are sealed," I promised, unable to stop myself from wrapping her in my arms and pressing loud kisses all over her face.

She wriggled and shrieked a protest, but all in all, it didn't seem like she was trying all that hard to get away from me.

I cleaned up the kitchen, and then it was time to start getting ready. Once my makeup was on and the loaves were done, I decided to take a picture of the finished product and send it to Seth. Almost immediately my phone buzzed for close to a minute straight with all the emojis and gifs he sent. *Well, now I guess I* have *to bring him some,* I thought, grinning to myself. My grin dimmed a little though as I thought about how he'd probably not had much of that in his childhood, from the things he'd already told me. Even my mother, cold and critical as she'd been, had occasionally made me cookies or a cake for my birthday.

Ninety minutes of primping later I was pulling my car into the parking lot and trying not to think too much about how I looked. Wearing dresses was always a stressful experience, paranoia about my scars showing blasting through my mind the entire time, but since Seth was taking me to a bistro instead of a pizza parlor it felt more appropriate to wear something…well, *dressy*. When it was warm out, there was another layer to it, because I also couldn't shave my armpits or my upper legs thanks to having HS. Shaving, plucking, and waxing all irritated my volatile skin, and the last time I'd caved to peer pressure and shaved my legs all the way up I'd wound up with a breakout near the crease where my leg met my hip that was so bad I'd had to call off work and have the damn things lanced. Couldn't move my leg for a week without pain.

How to bring up my skin issues was my biggest concern. Would he still want to be with me knowing what my thighs looked like, after seeing the puckered red scars under my breasts and in my armpits? I knew it was a lot to take in. It was so bad that it eclipsed my insecurities about other things, like the way my tummy and breasts looked after having a child or the fact that I was starting to get fine lines and grays.

This time parking was no problem, and I was the one waiting by the front door. I had pulled out my phone to send a quick text letting Seth know I was there when a sharp whistle cut through my thoughts and I blinked, coming back into myself in a rush. My eyes darted around, trying to find the source of the noise, only to spot Seth walking up to the front of the restaurant, his tawny skin gleaming in the sun and his gold eyes trained on me standing near the bistro's clapboard, devouring me with his gaze. He stopped in front of me, his hands shoved into the pockets of his gray skinny jeans and his chest straining against the fabric of his black button-up.

"Hey, gorgeous," he purred, making heat and want pool in my belly. "You look good enough to eat," he added, leaning a little closer to me and grinning wolfishly.

"You're just saying that because the dress pattern looks like sprinkles," I giggled, my face flaming hot and my heart in my throat even as my nipples pricked to attention.

He chuckled, taking my hand and threading our fingers together to lead us into the restaurant. "I can't lie to you, Eva: it *is* a factor." A strange expression crossed his face, but it was gone as soon as it appeared, to be replaced by another brilliant smile. "But you're also just a very attractive person. And pink suits you."

I returned his smile, warmth suffusing me. "You look pretty good yourself, sir," I murmured as we got to the hostess counter.

"Reservation for Meyers," he told her, and she nodded, gesturing a server over to show us to our table.

Once we were seated I cracked open my menu and started perusing. "So, your name really is Seth Meyers, huh? Like the comedian?" I asked idly.

"What comedian?"

I looked up at him. "I think he was on SNL. He might have a talk show, too? I don't know, he's someone I see around but I don't really follow him or anything." I pulled out my phone and googled the name. "Yeah, see? This guy." I turned the phone so he could see the picture I'd pulled up. Seth looked blankly at my phone then shrugged.

"No idea who that is."

My brow scrunched. "Really? You haven't seen him around? No one's ever commented on it?" He shook his head.

"So then you must have gotten the Mike Meyers jokes. Or *Michael* Meyers, the movie monster guy. People are so weird like that." Oh god I was rambling, but I couldn't seem to stop. "Like, you happen to have a name *kind* of like a famous person's so people assume that you *must* be related to them. It happened to my friend Aisha Freeman in high school. 'Oh, what's it like being related to god?' Dumb jokes like that. 'Cause of the movie." Shit, I was really on a tear. And starting to sweat like crazy.

Seth just continued to look at me kind of blankly. After a second he shrugged again. "Nope, you're the first to make the connection. You want to get any appetizers to start?" He pointed at something on the menu with a thick finger. "Bruschetta sounds good."

I shook off the strange moment, too glad that he wasn't giving me shit for the word vomit to press him on his name. It was silly to let myself get so worked up over it, anyway. I smiled at him and hoped he wouldn't notice the sweat I could feel beading in my cleavage. "Yeah, it does sound good," I agreed, taking a desperate gulp of my water. Was I messing this up? It was so hard to tell sometimes, with how what was consider polite seemed to constantly shift and mutate.

There was nothing quite like thinking a social interaction had gone well only to discover after the fact they thought you were weird and would rather not talk to you ever again.

But the strange moment did get me thinking about his past—or rather, how little I knew about it. I was only a little ashamed to admit I'd looked him up, and while I'd found nothing alarming I hadn't entirely trusted that. He *did* share a name with a celebrity, after all. And Seth Meyers might not even be his real name.

Once the server had come and taken our orders I leaned closer, folding my hands together and giving him a bright smile. Then, in a desperate attempt to not get my heart shattered into a million pieces down the line, I decided to hell with it and asked what I wanted to know: "So. What crimes have you committed?"

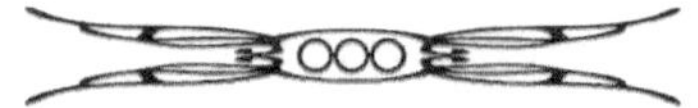

<u>SEPHYR</u>

I swear, my heart stopped dead in my chest. *This woman.*

All I could manage was flopping my mouth open and closed like a dying fish. "S...sorry?"

Eva smiled apologetically. "Well, I was thinking about it, and while I don't care what sorts of stuff you've done all that much for *me*, I have to think of my daughter, too, and make sure I'm not bringing anyone dangerous into her life. You hear horror stories about it all the time and I'd just…like to know I've done my best to avoid it." If I wasn't so horrified I'd think she was real cute right now, with her hands fluttering in front of her and her chest and neck gone beet red. Hell, who was I kidding; it was *still* cute.

My mouth had gone dry, but I was too frozen in shock to grab my water and gulp some down. I had to tread really carefully here. It didn't make any sort of sense, but I wanted to be honest with her. Something deep inside of me was sick and horrified at the thought of lying to her, of deceiving her any more than I already was. "I can understand that," I said slowly. "And if I want this to go somewhere then you should know this stuff. Which I very much do! Want this to go somewhere, that is," I added hastily, remembering how I'd nearly bungled the date last night by not being careful enough with what I said. "It's kind of hard for me to talk about though. I'm not...I'm not proud of that part of my life." It was a shock to realize that that was true: I wasn't exactly ashamed of what I'd had to do to survive—because, y'know, it had *worked,* right?—but I wasn't proud of it.

Her face softened, and she reached out to me, laying her hand on my arm. I clutched at her with my other hand, wanting to feel the warmth of her skin against mine. "I do understand, Seth. How when our backs are against the wall we sometimes have to do ugly things to survive. I guess...what I'm really asking is if you did things to hurt other people just to cause hurt. If you were cruel. Maybe I'm crazy, but it's the cruelty that scares me. Hurting someone or taking advantage just because you can, or because it feels good...*that's* what's scary."

I should have just told her what she wanted to hear and been done with it. But instead, I actually thought about it, excavating ancient memories to turn them over, to peer at them more closely than I had in years. Maybe ever.

"Can't honestly say I've never been cruel," I admitted quietly, clutching at her hand like it was my lifeline. "Especially when I was a kid. I was...*vrakaash,* I was so *angry.* Didn't know what to do with it all." I'd picked a lot of fights when I was young, had gone out of my way to scare people and terrorize those I'd felt had wronged me. I'd picked on the few kids who were smaller than me, taking their stuff just because I could. But there was a line I didn't cross, that I could admit freely to Eva and still be telling the whole truth. "But I never had sex with anyone who wasn't a fully consenting adult. Or at least a peer." I grinned sheepishly. "I was kind of a slut as a teen. But not too stupid to not use protection." After what had happened with Billieu—back-to-back pandemics including one that had been sexually transmitted—most people took safe sex seriously, even degenerates like me and the people I'd hung around with. "And while I can't say I never hurt anyone..." I licked my lips, the urge to close my eyes or just break the intense eye contact I was having with Eva growing almost too strong to resist. But I gritted my teeth and toughed it out. "It was never in cold blood. Only ever did it for survival. To people who were at least as bad as me." Even in the contracts I'd taken, I'd avoided anything that targeted a normal person who'd just happened to piss off an asshole with too much money.

Eva looked a little stricken, but she didn't pull away from me, and she didn't look disgusted with me. Hope poked a tender green shoot out of the blasted soil deep inside me. I'd been sure she would have backed away from me, left the bistro screaming never to see me again. But even if she didn't look happy, she was still here, still holding my hand, squeezing it like she was comforting me.

She offered me a small smile, making that little green sprout of hope stand a little taller. "Thank you for telling me. For being honest. It's a lot to process but...I think I can live with that."

My brows shot up, my third eye opening almost painfully wide beneath my helix skin. "Are you serious?" I asked, incredulous.

Eva flushed, looking embarrassed. "I'm not stupid," she snapped, yanking her hand back and crossing her arms over her chest. "And I don't *like* it. But it's not bad enough that I'm worried about Maggie. If I started dating someone and they hurt her, or if they hurt me and left her all alone in this world...That's what I'm worried about, and big picture? You stealing stuff and picking fights and taking out scumbags isn't...the worst, I guess."

"I'm sorry, Eva. I didn't mean it like that. It's just...you're so damn *good*. You're one of the kindest people to ever give me the time of day and I honestly thought that that would be it, just now." I licked my lips, finally snapping out of my stupor enough to take a shaky sip of my water.

Just then the server reappeared with our appetizer and drinks, telling us our meal would be out shortly. I smiled and thanked her, but I wanted to pick her up and chuck her across the room for interrupting our conversation.

Once we were alone again I reached for Eva's hand and felt overwhelming relief when she took it, studying my face. "I promise you, on my soul and anything else you want me to swear it on, that I'll never hurt you or Maggie. I know we only just met but I already care about the both of you. I know you have no reason to believe me but... I do."

I couldn't read the look on her face. "You know, it's kind of crazy...but I trust you. I believe you. Not just because I want to because you're so hot—" she cut herself off, her chest and neck flaring with color. I couldn't help the smirk that settled on my face. "Anyway, not because of that, but because something about you makes me feel like I can. Is that crazy? Should I be running screaming for the hills?"

"No, no I...I feel the same way. From the minute I saw you I felt like I could be myself with you, like I could—" I cut myself off, shocked to my core that that thought had even entered my mind—that I could *love* her. People like me had a hard time falling in love. And we definitely didn't get to have other people fall in love with *us*. "...Like I could build something with you." There, that sounded more normal. And it was true, even if it wasn't quite the whole story.

The smile she shot me was so sweet it ached. I felt like I was going to melt into a puddle from how warm and gorgeous she was with just that one little smile. Did she know how powerful it was? Something told me she didn't, and that made it all the more beautiful. I smiled back, and the tension building between us finally broke, both of us reaching for a piece of bruschetta.

"Sorry I'm so bad at dates," she apologized between bites of her food. "First I make you hang out with my kid, then I grill you half to death out of nowhere."

"Don't forget that we met because I rendered a free service to you in an emergency situation."

She narrowed her eyes at me, trying her best to glare, but the corners of her mouth twitched and I could tell I'd gotten away with it. I mean, if my past hadn't scared her away then what were the chances that a little bit of teasing was going to be what did me in?

I still couldn't believe she was cool with it. And I *really* couldn't believe that I'd actually *told* her all that. I'd never told anyone anything that personal in my whole life. I wasn't the kind of guy to just offer up what I was thinking and feeling on a silver platter. I didn't just...*tell* people things. Yet here I was, spilling my guts to this odd but utterly charming Earth female.

Something about that niggled at the back of my head, like a memory that had gone paper-thin with time, but I was distracted by our entrées arriving, and the feeling vanished as quickly as it'd come.

The more I learned about Eva the more I liked her. I liked that she kept her food completely separate on her plate. "Food segregation is the only one I support," she explained when I raised an eyebrow at her re-arranging her food, making me laugh. "I know it's weird; my mom hated how picky I was growing up."

She hadn't had a hard life like mine, but as we talked she revealed she had been a lonely child, often left out of activities with the other children and struggling to earn her parents' approval.

"I was a really weird kid," she said. "I had a lot of trouble making friends. I got along better with the parents of my classmates and my teachers than I did with the other kids my age. So I was off on my own, playing by myself a lot. I started baking as a way to comfort myself and it just sort of...turned into a lifelong obsession."

"If I would have been here when I was a kid I'd've been your friend," I told her, smiling at her.

She laughed, looking at me from under her eyelashes. "I don't know, I was *really* weird. Like, talking to myself and playing with garbage weird."

"Playing with garbage is underrated. Some of the most fun I've had is playing with stuff someone else decided to toss. We'd've been *best* friends, eating cupcakes and playing with trash like a couple of vermin."

She laughed loudly, throwing her head back. "Oh my *god*, the mental picture from that!" She dabbed at the tears smearing the makeup along her undereyes. "It's nice to finally meet another trash goblin. You'll be relieved to hear that the apple did not fall far from the tree and Maggie likes spending her free time turning trash into art." A wistful expression settled on her face, topped off with a soft, warm smile that made me ache. "She's really good. She has this thing that she's making from soda tabs that looks like chainmail; very cool stuff."

"I'd love to see it." And I meant that. "She's a really great kid." Even though it was fast, I'd begun wondering what it would be like to join with Eva, to mate myself to her in the human way and adopt her cub as my own. We'd raise Maggie together, get to know each other better on our own time, no clocks ticking, no Serr'eza lingering in the back of my mind and demanding my time. For the first time, I was within sight of being able to have a normal happy life, full of love and comfort, full of light and joy. No more running. I might not even have to hide who I was, if Eva continued being this understanding and caring.

My throat closed painfully at the thought, at how beautiful but completely impossible it was. I cleared my throat and smiled at Eva, who was watching me. "Sorry," I told her. "Spaced out. So, tell me Eva; if you love baking so much then why do you work in a call center?"

Her mouth twisted into a sad frown. "Because I have Maggie. I'm raising her all by myself, and she's had a hard enough time due to some personal stuff it's not really my place to say. I bake in my free time for the people I care about, and that's still wonderful. Like I said before, opening up my own bakery is just too risky."

I frowned. "But it's your passion. Isn't that worth a little risk?"

"Oh, yes," she told me, stirring her drink absently. "All the best things in life are risky. But it's one thing to risk yourself and something else entirely to risk the happiness and safety of your child. I'm not *just* Eva; I'm Maggie's mom, too."

Quit your job, I wanted to tell her. *Quit it right now, anyone can see it makes you miserable. Let me take care of you instead. Then you can take all the risks you want because I'll be there to catch you if you stumble.* But I didn't say any of that. Instead, I just smiled sadly, holding her hand tight.

As much as I wanted to stay like that with her forever, tucked safe into this little bubble of time where none of the *vrakaash* in our lives was there to pull us apart, eventually Eva told me she had to go to make sure Maggie was okay and get dinner started.

I wished she'd ask me to come over.

After I paid the bill I walked her to her car, not wanting our time together to end just yet.

"Tell Maggie I'm sorry for keeping you out so long," I told her as we stopped and faced each other outside her silver sedan. "Then tell her I was just kidding and I'd keep you out longer if I could."

Eva laughed, swaying ever so slightly closer to me in the process. Heat swept through me, my skin tingling with awareness until my fur was all standing on end under my helix skin. I swallowed, whatever dumb thing I'd been about to say dying in my throat. The rest of the world faded away, the only thing I could possibly see Eva's stormy eyes, wide and gleaming, her pink lips parted gently. Her scent wrapped around me, calling to me, tethering her to me, singing in my blood. I swallowed, but the lump in my throat kept me breathless.

I let gravity do its work and let my body drift closer to

hers, my hand coming up and tucking a stray lock of her dark hair behind her ear.

"Can I kiss you?" I heard myself asking, my voice so full of gravel I barely recognized myself.

She licked those pink lips of hers, drawing my eye and making me ache with want for her. "Yes," she breathed, and that was all I needed.

I pressed myself in tight against her, cupping her oval face in my hands as I bent to press my lips to hers.

Her kiss was everything I'd hoped it would be and still somehow *more*. She was sweetness and softness, warmth and light, but she wasn't timid or afraid. She didn't shrink from me or let me lead; she took the reins and showed me what she wanted and I'd be damned if that wasn't the hottest fucking thing I'd ever experienced. My hands slid from her face, one carding through her hair to cradle the back of her head and the other drifting down to the small of her back to coax her even closer. I needed her heat seeping into my skin like her scent was soaking into my blood. I devoured her, teasing her lips further apart so I could slide my tongue into her mouth and taste her from the source.

I couldn't stop the groan that ripped from my throat at the silky feel of my tongue gliding into her mouth, tasting me as much as I was tasting her. I realized her hands were fisting the front of my shirt, gripping the fabric tight, but as our tongues danced together her hands flattened, smoothing over my chest and just grazing the piercing I had in my left nipple. I couldn't tell if she knew what she was touching, but just that tiny brush of her little finger had me thinking I might just spend in my pants like a cub.

She groaned low in her throat, angling her hips so that the

stunning heat between her legs was pressing into my hip, grinding into me in a way that had me wanting to howl like a fucking animal. My hand on her lower back slid lower, palming her ass. Eva whimpered into my mouth, her cunt pressing harder into me and making my cock and sleeve throb hard in my pants. Just a couple of thin layers of fabric were all that was standing in the way of being able to claim her right now, for all the world to see that this female was *mine.*

She ripped her mouth from mine, her pink lips swollen and wet and looking good enough to eat, then looked around the parking lot to check if anyone was watching.

"You want some privacy?" I asked, my voice so rough it was unrecognizable. "We could get in the car."

She bit her lip, considering, before breaking out into a wide grin and nodding.

I grinned back, pressing a quick kiss to her lips before she dug around in her purse for her keys. The car doors unlocked with a beep, then she yanked the door open and slid into the backseat, tugging me in behind her. I huffed a laugh, wiggling around until I was sitting in the middle of the bucket seat, then I pulled her into my lap. She straddled me, her knees on either side of my hips, and my hands went straight to her thighs, sliding under the hem of her skirt to caress the soft skin there.

"Can I touch you?" I asked, leaving my hands down by her knees just in case she wasn't feeling it. But she just let out a breathy sigh, rolling her hips towards me in a silent request. But I wasn't having any of that. "Yes or no, gorgeous?"

"Yes. Please," she panted, ripping one of my hands from her leg and pressing it into her breast. I sucked in a breath, the soft warmth of her flesh the most holy thing I'd ever experienced, and then I was kissing her again, one hand kneading and tweaking her ripe mound of flesh while the other slid up to the apex of her thighs, seeking the liquid heat of her sex.

Fuck, she's so wet. She'd soaked clean through her panties, what felt like cotton clinging to every fold of her. I wanted to taste her, to make her come against my mouth over and over until she was too sensitive, but now wasn't the time. We were technically in public, and it was a good idea to keep clothes on, even if her windows were tinted.

I ran my finger along the seam of her through her wet panties, making her shiver and gasp. I slipped my hand under the waistband, sliding my finger into her crease and circling her clit with light strokes. She mewled into my mouth, her whole body shuddering as I continued to work her swollen bud. Her head fell back, the most beautiful little moans coming out of her as I worked her slowly, her pelvis pressing into my finger, trying to coax me faster.

I leaned forward and nibbled at her throat, getting drunk on the smell of her skin, on the perfume of her cunt filling the enclosed space of her car. Fuck, she smelled so good she was making my mouth water. I slid my fingers lower, until I was just pressing on her entrance, circling it like I had her clit. "This still alright?" I asked in between kisses to her pulsepoint.

"Yessir," she breathed, her fingers digging into my shoulders.

I sank my fingers into her wet channel, her inner walls clamping down on me, sucking me in deeper. My dick pulsed in my pants, throbbing hard as I imagined what it would be like to sink into her, her juices mingling with mine and soaking us both. My sleeve clenched on nothing, precum and my natural lubricant mixing and gluing my underwear to my skin. I rocked my fingers into her, crooking them and looking for that spot I'd read so much about, while I used my thumb to keep working her clit.

Eva cried out, her eyes squeezing shut as she rode my hand, making the car sway. Anyone who walked by would know exactly what was going on in here, but I couldn't have cared less; not with this gorgeous creature in front of me, looking so goddamn beautiful and using *my* hand to get her pleasure. Those sounds she was making were because of me, were *for* me, and I captured her lips with mine again so I could drink them down. I'd never get my fill of them, I could tell already.

Her cries reached a fever pitch, her hips rocking into my hand even as I pumped in and out of her, and then she froze, curling forward even as her cunt clamped down around my fingers and her inner walls and clit throbbed and fluttered in tandem. She buried her face in my neck, screaming her pleasure into my skin so it was muffled.

"That's it, Eva," I crooned, slowing my movements but not stopping, wanting to wring out every drop of this orgasm for her. "You did so good, gorgeous."

She ground into my hand a few more times, her pussy still pulsing weakly, until she must have gotten too sensitive and eased herself off of me.

I brought my hand to my mouth, licking myself clean with a deep groan while she watched me, wide-eyed. She was flushed deep pink, her skin dewy with sweat and looking deliciously rumpled. My sex gave another hard twitch in my pants as her tangy flavor burst on my tongue.

"Delicious," I drawled, making her flush deepen. Was I coming on too strong? I was decent at getting a female into bed, but I'd never tried to keep one around before. I'd never tried to...*build* something with them.

I watched her face as the haze of lust lifted and she came back into herself. I reached out and cupped the back of her head, drawing her in for another kiss. This time it was slower, sweeter, like she was trying to memorize me with her lips and tongue. My heart started pounding for a whole new reason, my achingly hard cock fading from my awareness as I fell into Eva, sinking deeper and deeper into her until I was dizzy, drunk on her sweet mouth and her soft sighs.

It was easily the best kiss of my life and I didn't want it to end. It felt like I might just die if we stopped kissing, if I had to breathe air that I wasn't sharing with her, if I had to go back to my house that didn't have a single whiff of her scent.

But the kiss did end, and I had to put my big boy pants on and put myself back together after she'd ripped me right apart with those tiny little hands of hers. Now that I'd had this little taste of her I'd never be able to walk away, no matter what Serr'eza or his people tried to do to me.

"I should really get going. I've already been gone longer than I told Maggie I'd be."

I nodded and helped her straighten herself out, finger-combing her hair for her to fix where I'd mussed it and smoothing her clothes back into place. Then she climbed off me and hopped out of the car, me following once I'd adjusted myself in my pants to be less obvious.

"I had a fantastic time," I told her honestly, snatching one of her hands and pressing lingering kisses to her knuckles. "Text me when you get home?"

She smiled, emotion lighting up those big gray eyes of hers and making them glow. "Yeah, I will. I had a great time, too." She flushed red, making the direction of her thoughts crystal clear. "Bye, Seth," she whispered, ripping my heart right out of my chest. It was time to go, and I was just going to have to ignore the beast howling inside me to sling her over my shoulder and run away with her.

"Goodbye, Eva," I rasped, stepping back to give her space. "Drive safe, gorgeous," I added.

"I will." She had her car door open and was most of the way seated when she froze. "Oh! I almost forgot to give you this!" She slipped back out of the car, digging around in her purse and removing something wrapped in cling film that she handed to me.

I took it, my heart twisting painfully in my chest and the faint scent of sugar and banana wafted up to me. "Is this that bread you showed me earlier?"

She nodded, biting her kiss-swollen lip. "Yeah. You were just so excited—"

I pulled her to me with a groan, unable to stop myself from claiming another kiss from her. "Thank you. So much."

She laughed softly, avoiding my eyes. "It's just some banana bread, you maniac."

"Don't you 'just' me. You made this with your own two hands and it both looks and smells delicious. I'm—I'm honored to get to have this."

Her eyes finally slid up to mine, something soft and tender there that made me ache with want. I wanted to spend the rest of my days looking into those stormcloud eyes and steeping in her sweetness. "Okay," she murmured, easing my thoughts out of their spiral. "I better go. Talk to you soon?"

"You better."

She slipped back into her car, staying there this time, and I retreated to the sidewalk so she could back out, waving at her when she glanced at me. Then she was driving away, and I was left standing in the parking lot second-guessing my whole damn life.

Chapter 8

Trusting Men is Always Dangerous

<u>EVA</u>

With the way that Seth had kissed me, I might as well have never been kissed before in my life. It was toe-curling, knee-liquifying, panty-meltingly intense. And the way he'd *touched* me…

I'd only just met the guy and I was already addicted to him.

In some ways, it felt like I'd known him for way longer than I had. He hit all my buttons, even ones I'd had no idea existed, in a way that was almost overwhelming. A part of me was weirdly glad that he had a troubled past. It was proof he wasn't perfect, and that made me feel more at ease. And there were those brief flashes of insecurity I kept seeing. As a deeply insecure person myself, I found it comforting to see it in others, taking it as proof that there were others like me out there finding it all difficult. It made him sweeter, softer in a way that made me desperate for more of him.

I sat in my car for a while after I pulled up in front of my house, taking deep breaths of the air that still smelled like sex even though I'd driven the whole way home with the windows down, trying to calm my revved-up body. I felt extremely awkward about waltzing into the house turned on and flustered. Knowing Mags, she'd somehow pick up on it right away and I'd have no choice but to fire myself into the sun out of embarrassment.

Finally feeling more or less calm and collected, I stepped out of my car and headed inside, my face heating when the movement brought just how wet and swollen I still was to my attention.

Maggie was in the kitchen grabbing a snack when I walked in. "Hey, Mommers," she singsonged, shoving an entire Oreo cookie into her mouth at once. "How was your date with Hot Stuff?"

I laughed. "Since when are you calling him 'Hot Stuff'? "

She shrugged. "Just trying it out. You're hot for each other and he's a redhead. I think it's fun."

"Well, please ask him before you call him anything but his name to his face. You don't want to be rude, right? Some people get bullied for being redheads, so he might be sensitive about your calling attention to it."

She nodded, looking thoughtful. "You right, you right." She sat at the little kitchen table we used for our meals and swept her hand at the empty seat across from herself. "Please begin the play-by-play. I crave it, Mother."

I laughed, feeling myself flush. "It was lunch, we talked..." *He finger-fucked me in the backseat of my car like we were horny teens…* "...what else is there to say?"

She squawked indignantly. "Umm, how about did you kiss? Did he get sloppy on you and show you a good time? How am I supposed to learn about romance and relationships if you don't spill the tea?"

I felt my face flaming, but I had to admit she had a point.

Kids learned by modeling and since I'd had no partner the entire time she'd been alive this was the first time I'd be able to model for her. Guilt stabbed through me. Had I been hurting her development this whole time? I'd thought I was protecting her, but was I?

"Alright, I will give you the PG deets, insolent child," I told her with a sigh. "But I want to change first, alright?"

"Fair," she allowed, eating another cookie.

I retreated to my room and peeled off my clothes. Everything was embarrassingly damp, between my nervous sweating and intense arousal. I happily donned my pajamas, then rejoined Maggie in the kitchen. I felt more like myself after the clothing change; less flustered and hyper-aware of my body.

I sat with a sigh, tapping my fingers on the tabletop in my excitement. "It was both very fun and very informative. I...I like Seth a lot. What are your thoughts about him so far?"

She shrugged, rolling the half-empty sleeve of cookies over the table. "I like him. He's not full of himself and he's *just* the right amount of idiot." We both laughed and I stole a cookie and took a big bite.

"Ouch, poor Seth. *Definitely* don't say that to his face." I snapped off another bite of my cookie and chewed it thoughtfully. "But I'm glad you like him. I want you to like anyone that I bring into your life. His track record isn't flawless, but he's a good guy. And...he's a *really* good kisser."

Maggie squealed and flapped her hands. "Oh my god, so you *did* kiss?!"

"Yes, and it was amazing. We'd been talking for a while before that, sharing all this stuff about our pasts, so it was very romantic."

She sighed, smiling dreamily. But after a moment something shifted, and her smile fell. "You think I'll ever find something like that?"

I felt like I'd been gutted. "Oh, honey…" I took her hand, squeezing it tight. "Yes. I think you absolutely will find someone who loves the crap out of you." There wasn't a doubt in my mind that she'd have no problem finding people who'd adore her and wouldn't give a single shit about the fact that she was trans. But I also wanted to be honest with her. "But it might take a little longer. Obviously, as a cis woman I can only know so much about what it's like being you, being young and trans, but even if it *is* a little harder, it won't be for forever. I just know you're gonna rock someone's socks off someday."

She smiled weakly. "Yeah, that's what I've been worried about. I wish people would just *see* me. See that I'm—I'm *just* me. I'm not…I'm not a freak."

"No, you are *not. At all.*" My throat got tight, concern for Maggie eclipsing my high from Seth. "I'm sorry you have it so much harder, baby. If I could make it better for you I would in a *heartbeat.*"

"I know. It's okay, Mom. I'm just…having a weird day, I guess." She used the tip of a finger to push crumbs around on the tabletop, her black nail polish badly chipped. "And at least I have you. A bunch of my online friends are still hiding because their parents aren't as cool."

I smiled weakly, my heart shattering. I wished I could adopt every single one of those kids. "God, that breaks my heart," I said softly. "But you're right; I know it's not the same, but you *do* have me. Always, monkey."

I got to my feet and wrapped my arms around her

shoulders, pulling her in for a hug. "Are you sure you're okay?"

She nodded, hugging me back. "Yeah."

I pulled away with one last squeeze and a kiss on her cheek.

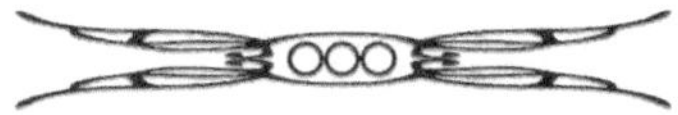

I'd always kept it to myself, not wanting to make myself an easy target to my teenager's teasing, but I'd always wondered why people would get so attached to their phones that they never let them out of their sight, sometimes even keeping them in their hands constantly, like they couldn't *stand* not touching them.

But out of nowhere, I'd become one of those people: glued to my phone, twitching every time I got a notification. Every ping that rang out, I prayed it would be from Seth. And lucky for me, it usually was.

It seemed like freelance security guards had an awful lot of time on their hands because unless he was asleep it never took more than an hour to get a response from him. Or maybe it was more like my situation and he was sneaking time on his phone when he should have been working. I had to admit it had made my week much less boring and grim to be able to spend my downtime chatting with him. He'd been showing me a lot of clips from his favorite movies, and getting me into the comics he liked so much, and I'd been sharing some of my choice meme cache with him and telling him all about my adventures with my sourdough starter—which was still doing well, thank you very much.

It was almost like he was genuine in his attraction to me

and legitimately wanted to date me. Crazy, right? But the more I talked to Seth, the more I believed that he was actually that into me.

Now it was about halfway through my day on Friday, and I was wondering if he'd want to get together again and do something over the weekend. My phone buzzed beside me on the table, and when I hung up with my current customer I took a moment to check my messages.

Seth: Hey, you're a gorgeous and intelligent woman of excellent taste, he'd written, making me wiggle in my seat and let out some *very* unladylike squeals.
Seth: I'm trying to impress someone but I'm having trouble coming up with date ideas that are suitably impressive. Thoughts?

I sent him an emoji of someone stroking their face while they pondered.

Me: Well dinner dates have been working out well so far.

My phone buzzed again, the chat thread updating with a gif of someone wiggling their eyebrows like their life depended on it.

Seth: Glad to hear you think so. But this lady is real special. And I want to take her somewhere fun. I get the impression she doesn't cut loose as often as she should.

Busted. I had to set my phone down again to take another call, and when I was done I had more adorable texts to sink my teeth into.

Seth: What's something you haven't done in a while that you miss? Something where you couldn't stop laughing and had to take at least a LITTLE nap after.

I laughed, throwing my head back. How was he so…in *tune* with me? My instinct was to pick something easy that wouldn't have any chance of annoying him…but that was fucking stupid, I realized. What was it that Magdalena had said before we went to Leonie's? *If he can't handle you at your casual pizza date then he doesn't deserve you at your MET Gala red carpet look.* From the mouth of babes, ammirite?

I smiled when I realized what it was that fit his criteria.

Me: The last time I had fun like that was just before I got pregnant with Maggie. Me and my friends went to an adult arcade and made ourselves sick on cheap pizza and too many video games that triggered motion sickness.

After that, it was a little more than half an hour before I was able to check my phone again. Seth had sent me links to several different options, making me melt. I liquefied still further, impossibly, when in another five minutes he'd told me he was taking "his girls" out after I was done with work and wouldn't take no for an answer. I mean, who *said* things like that?

It was the longest four hours of my life, but finally, *finally,* I was off the clock and free to do what I wanted through the weekend. Maggie had already been home for a couple of hours and seemed just as excited as me to be going out tonight.

I hurried up and changed, putting on comfy jeans and my favorite shirt at the moment, of a cartoon raccoon holding a Molotov cocktail and the words "Become Ungovernable" emblazoned on the front. I threw my hair up in a ponytail and threw on some sneakers. Then we were out the door to meet Seth at the arcade.

Seth swaggered into the arcade's lobby looking like a snack, as usual, wearing the crap out of a black henley and some gray jeans, the bottoms tucked into black combat-style boots that were very well-worn. "Hey, gorgeous," he greeted me with a grin, giving me a chaste peck on the lips that nonetheless had me feeling hot and breathless. "Mags," he greeted my daughter, clapping her on the shoulder affectionately. I was glad he hadn't tried to hug her; she wasn't overly fond of physical contact from most people.

We filed in, settling into the line to buy our cards and load them up with the points we'd need to play the games. Seth asked Maggie about school and paid genuine attention to her (admittedly) meandering tales of high school woe. She'd been struggling a lot with her English lit class, she was saying, because she hated the material they were having her read.

"Like, there *has* to be something besides *Lord of the Flies* that they could have us read to speculate on our inherent humanity and whether we band together or fight each other when society collapses. It's so pessimistic and gross for no reason, like Goldman was trying to show off some shit he'd thought of that *he* thought was really deep but it was actually just pure edgelord nonsense."

I laughed. It had been a while since I'd had to read it, but from what little I remembered, what she was saying made a kind of sense. And it *was* pretty crazy that my child was reading the same books I'd had to read nearly two decades ago. "'Hot Takes with Magdalena Nadzija', everyone," I teased, referring to a running joke we had. "Did you have to read that one, Seth?" I asked.

He looked uncomfortable for a moment before his face slid into another of his delicious grins. "Nah, I don't think I did. Sounds like I lucked out, huh?"

Maggie agreed, launching into part two of her rant about William Goldman's classic, while Seth's reaction to such an innocent question niggled at me. Was he hiding something from me? Was this one of the signs of something being wrong that my damn overly excited heart had missed? Or was I looking for trouble where there wasn't any? Maybe he'd had trouble with school. Maybe he hadn't finished, and it was a sore subject. That was perfectly reasonable, especially if he'd been raised here in the US. I still hadn't been able to place his accent, but there was something of a Southern twang to it sometimes, so it was possible.

I mentally shook myself, forcing my attention back on Seth and Maggie, who had moved on to talking about her loathsome English lit teacher. I couldn't seem to decide if my level of paranoia was too much or too little; on the one hand, everything I'd seen from Seth had been a dream come true: he was sweet, thoughtful, funny, nerdy, and great with my kid. On the other, there were some serious red flags in his past, and even if he wasn't currently a criminal—and as a security guard he was technically on the right side of the law now— did that mean I had nothing to worry about? I was too sheltered and privileged for this kind of analysis, I feared, and I'd have to just keep being vigilant.

Our loaded cards finally in hand, we wandered the arcade floor in search of a game that stood out to us. I tended to gravitate towards non-video games because too much light and movement messed with my head, but the last time I'd taken Maggie to the kiddie version of a place like this she'd been obsessed with the racing games where you hopped into a little plastic car seat and had to actually steer and stuff. I'd tried to get a feel for what kinds of games Seth liked while we'd been texting earlier, but he'd never been anywhere like this before. Now he stared at all of the flashing lights and boisterous signs, his mouth slightly agape as his eyes roved all over the machines, the people milling about, the prize center looming against a far wall with insane prizes dangling from the ceiling on plastic chains.

"This place is both one of the most amazing and horrible things I've ever seen," he breathed, holding my hand tight like he was afraid I'd slip away if he didn't. "What is that smell? It's like…old sweat?"

I laughed, patting his back. "It probably is. Who knows when the last time they cleaned this carpet was?" Seth shot me a look of horror, picking one of his boots up off the floor and inspecting the bottom like he'd be able to see the decades of bacteria baked into the worn fabric. "Just focus on the nice food smells, babe," I assured him, not realizing what I'd said until I noticed he was looking at me with a blend of surprise and satisfaction on his face.

"*You* smell pretty good," he purred, leaning in closer to me. "I think I'll just focus on that." *Lord help me, why is this man so* hot?!, I thought desperately, letting myself sway into him, his solid warmth soaking into my skin.

"Air hockey!" Maggie called, darting off to the left. "Mom,

rematch!" I laughed, tugging Seth along as we swooped in on the only free table in the little corral of them. She was already stretching and limbering up by the time I'd made it over, the intense seriousness of her expression at odds with the silly little characters painted all over the table. "I'm going to get you this time," she promised, settling into a ready stance.

I choked back a laugh, going to set my purse down on the floor only for Seth to snatch it from me and look at me like I was insane—I suppose given his feelings about the floor that made sense. I smiled at him gratefully, touched by his thoughtfulness and thinking there was no way a guy like this could be bad for me. I grabbed my paddle and settled into a stance mirroring Maggie's, making a *bring it on* motion with my hand.

Normally I had zero hand-eye coordination and slow reflexes—but something about air hockey made sense to my body in a way that no other sports or games did, and it drove Maggie's competitive instincts *nuts*. She could beat me at just about every other game—but not air hockey.

It was a close game, but in the end, I managed to snatch a win from her, making her growl and hop around in frustration. "Best of three!" she demanded, one hand flapping in irritation.

"I don't know, baby. You're getting awfully riled up from just the one game." I didn't mind it, knowing that like me, she just needed to calm herself down by letting off some steam, but in such a crowded place there were going to be a lot of people who *did* mind, and it would kill me to see her wilt and hide away something that was only natural for her. *What if Seth sees it and gets weirded out?*, I found myself wondering, and that one hurt more than I'd've thought. Because it was something that I often needed to do, too; I'd gone my whole life hiding it, but if I was going to be with someone they'd see it eventually. Would it freak him out? Would he be cool with my scars only to find some of my weirder traits unsettling and strange?

"Mind if I step in and try?" Seth asked, watching us with soft amusement—including at Maggie's hopping.

"I have to pee, so you take my spot," Maggie offered, handing him her paddle. He took it with a polite nod of his head, then turned to me and speared me with one of his slow, sexy little grins. The crazy lights in here were making his piercings twinkle a kaleidoscope of colors, somehow making him even more beautiful.

"Have you ever played before?" I asked, squirming a little as my eyes trailed over his masculine curves and heat pooled low in my belly.

"Can't say I have, but I think I get it from watching you two. Just gotta slide into your hole, right?"

My cheeks flamed, a squeak of surprise flying up my throat. "It's called a *goal*," I hissed, licking my lips and darting my eyes around to see if anyone had heard.

"Oh, I know," he crooned, wiggling his eyebrows at me.

"Alright, smartass," I grumbled, but I couldn't help grinning back at him. "Flirting won't help you; I'll still kick your butt and have fun doing it."

He smirked, starting the new game up. "Alright, but you gotta buy me breakfast after."

I sputtered, completely unprepared for this level of flirting. Which was the only reason he managed to land a shot in my goal, his hand snapping out quick as lightning and slipping the puck past my defenses easily.

I frowned at him, narrowing my eyes as I scooped the puck out of my goal and set it back on the table. "Beginner's luck," I insisted.

"Whatever you say, gorgeous," he taunted, shooting me another smirk as he bounced on the balls of his feet like he was getting ready to box.

But it proved to be anything but beginner's luck: Seth had the reflexes of a cat, sinking shot after shot and stopping every attempt I made at returning the favor.

Just as Maggie walked back up to the table from her trip to the bathroom, Seth was sinking in the final goal, setting off the LED victory screen.

"Seth's on my team!" my daughter shouted, patting his shoulder in her excitement. Seth grabbed her hand and raised it in victory, whooping along with her and joining her in doing a victory lap around the table.

They were so adorable and goofy I couldn't help but laugh, bowing theatrically and conceding the victory. "Well played, I am defeated utterly," I intoned, snagging them around the neck and pressing a kiss to each of their cheeks. It was then that I realized that Seth still had my bag, slung over his shoulder so that it rested completely on his back. *Shit, he was even playing with a handicap.*

People were waiting for the table, so we agreed to leave it at a tie and move along, playing a few other games before hunger took hold and we agreed it was time for dinner. The little restaurant section was fairly crowded, but we were able to snag a small table in the middle of the floor. We ordered our drinks, Seth asking for a basket of mozzarella sticks to start, and we chatted quietly together about what games had been our favorites and what we'd seen that we might want to try playing afterward.

Once our orders were in I excused myself to use the bathroom, my bladder suddenly reminding me I hadn't relieved it in several hours *very* loudly. I slipped into the grimy restroom, my nose wrinkling at the reek of antiseptic and cheap air freshener, but there wasn't a line and I was done quickly, at least.

Overwhelmed by the strong smells and loud noises of the bathroom, I threw myself out the door a little recklessly and collided with a much larger body.

"Oh! I'm *so* sorry—"

"Hey girl, no worries. Not every day you get a gorgeous woman throwing herself at you."

I took in the person I'd collided with, noting that he stunk of cheap body spray almost as badly as the bathroom had. A hand grabbed my upper arm, pinning me in place where he could look at me. I yanked my arm free, noting his eyes were bloodshot and unfocused, and now that I was looking for it I could detect the sour reek of alcohol under the oppressive body spray. "I'm here with my boyfriend," I said firmly, backing away and dodging around him.

"Hey—hey come on, I'm just talking to you," he called, taking off after me and following me on my path back to my table and safety. I picked up my pace.

"That's cool, but I'm not interested!" I called over my shoulder. I caught a flash of bright copper curls and the tightness in my chest eased up just a fraction.

Persistent Drunk Guy caught up to me again, grabbing my arm and dragging me to a halt. "C'mon, just give me five minutes," he wheedled, yanking my arm closer to his body. "What can five minutes hurt?"

A pale, skinny hand crusted with rings latched onto Drunk Guy's wrist and tore him off of me. "Leave her alone, asshole!" Maggie shouted, drawing the eyes of most of the people nearby.

Seth stepped between us and my assailant, drawing himself up to his full height and puffing his chest out. "Just walk away, man," he growled low, the sound bordering on animal. Why was that having such a strong effect on me?

Persistent Drunk Guy smirked, looking down at Seth like he thought he was adorable. "What are you gonna do about it, shortstop?"

Seth took a step closer, crowding into Drunk Guy's space. "I'm just asking you to go back to whatever you were doing and mind your business. You really want to make a scene here, with all these kids around? You want the cops to get called? The lady is with me and she's not interested. So just walk away."

Drunk Guy's brow furrowed, his eyes darting around and noticing the audience that had formed for the first time. He snorted and shrugged, muttering something that was probably disrespectful before stumbling away, melding with the crowd.

Once it was obvious the show was over everyone dispersed, and Seth finally relaxed his shoulders, spinning to check me over and make sure I was okay. "Did he hurt you, gorgeous?" he murmured, tucking a loose strand of my hair behind my ear so he could get a better look at my face. "Do you want to leave?"

I shook my head, meeting his vivid gold eyes and breathing his scent deep into my lungs and feeling my racing heart settle. I leaned in and kissed him, throwing my arms around his neck in a brief but tight hug. "No, I'm alright. That asshole isn't worth letting our dinner get ruined over."

Seth squeezed me back, nuzzling the side of my face with his nose briefly, before releasing me and leading us back to our table.

Soon after our food arrived, the tension between us loosened and conversation started flowing more easily among us once more. But I found myself thinking back over that conflict again and again. Not because it had scared me—although I'd be lying if I said it hadn't gotten to me—but because of how Seth had reacted. He'd been calm, level-headed, and hadn't really threatened that guy. He'd put himself between me and him, and his body language had screamed intimidation, but despite all that he hadn't actually tried to hurt the guy at all. That wasn't the behavior of someone who was still as dangerous as their past implied, surely.

I felt something around my heart crumble away, letting that silly organ flutter and fly free in my chest.

Chapter 9

The Call

<u>SEPHYR</u>

I'd spent my week fabricating signs of progress for Serr'eza to keep him from getting any more antsy, but it had barely been enough.

"It has been too long, Kasdaan. Some sales receipts and inspection certificates aren't enough. I need *merchandise.*

"I've been patient with you, mutt. Naran'haa had nothing but good things to say about you from the job you took for him. But my patience is at its end. I need seven humans in my hands by the end of the month. It's what, two weeks to fly here from Earth? That leaves you with four days. So you better not have been jerking me around. I'll fucking find you, you *vrakaashaad.* And you'll wish that all I did was kill you by the time I'm done."

"Whatever, Serr'eza. Big talk from someone too scared to ever get his hands dirty. Don't worry, I'll deliver."

I was officially out of time, but I hadn't even *begun* to work up the courage to talk to Eva about it.

The way I figured it, I'd have to abandon everything here and flee as far as I could. I'd destroy everything the brotherhood lent me and lay some false trails for myself, for when they inevitably came looking for me. But the problem was, I wanted Eva and Maggie to come with me. Which was going to make running and hiding a thousand times harder. Neither of them had my kind of experience, and they had roots here in Chicago; roots that I didn't want them to have to tear up just for me. But they'd also set down roots in my heart, too, and as foolish and selfish as it was, I didn't want them to rip those out, either.

But how in the world would I bring that up? "Hey, Eva, quick question: I know you've only known me for a little while, but do you want to turn your back on everything you and your daughter know to live a life on the run from some horrifically awful people?"

I snatched my phone off of the table beside me with a huff, checking my notifications. I smiled, my foul mood improving when I saw a missed text from Eva.

Eva: I'm so bored today. You want to come over here and keep me company on my lunch break?

My breath stilled. She hadn't invited me into her home yet. We'd been meeting at our dates so far, then going our separate ways after. It was the middle of the day, and just for the duration of her lunch break, but it still moved me. It was such a small thing, but it solidified that no matter what, I couldn't just leave her behind. I swallowed, my throat feeling thick and my eyes curiously hot as I sent her a text back.

Me: Of course, I'd love to see you. What's your address so I can map it? After a second I added, *You want me to bring anything?*

She told me she didn't need anything but my company then sent me her address, and I was dressed and out the door with my helix skin on in under five minutes. She was close, only fifteen minutes away, less if I was a little reckless, and my heart was thundering against my ribs the entire drive. My hands had started shaking at some point, and it seemed like all the deep breaths in the world weren't going to make it stop.

"What the fuck is wrong with me?" I muttered, shaking my hands out at a stoplight. "It's just lunch. It's not even for that long, you *vrakaashaad*." But here I was feeling breathless and flushed like I was a cub about to get his first kiss. There was just something about the intimacy of knowing I was going to see her private home, where she lived and everything was suffused with her: her scent in the air, her tastes presented in the decor, her passions listed in the things that would be scattered around. I couldn't care less if I so much as hugged her, so long as I got that glimpse of her.

I pulled over an popped on my hazard lights. I threw my car into park and sucked in some deep breaths, doing the breathing exercises that had gotten me through this before.

Because somehow, for the first time in years, I was on the verge of having a panic attack. Ironic, considering that in a way panic attacks were what had gotten me to this point. But where was this coming from? Was it a delayed reaction to my conversation with Serr'eza? Was it knowing my relationship with Eva was about to change, to become more intimate? No —neither of those felt quite right.

But then it hit me: it was because a part of my knew I'd have to leave Eva, that I'd have to leave all of this behind. I didn't want to be cruel and drag her and Maggie with me, but I couldn't stay here. Serr'eza knew I was here, would send Siit'ron and anyone else he could to this city to find me when I went dark. Which meant my time with those two beautiful females was limited—and that limit was four days.

But then I went ice cold as another thought struck me: when he couldn't find me, would he somehow be able to find Eva and Maggie? Would he take them and hurt them to try and get to me, to draw me out?

"Fuck." I squeezed my eyes shut, feeling sick at the images that flitted through my mind.

There was no winning here. Not with me so invested and my two females so vulnerable. The *only* chance of keeping them safe was in bringing them with me. Could I charm Eva into doing that? Or would I have to just…take them, whether or not they wanted to go?

I swore again, then turned off my hazards and merged back into traffic. I pulled up to Eva's address a few minutes later, smiling at the cute little ranch-style home she shared with her daughter. I shoved my dark thoughts down deep, deciding that if those were my only two options then my first step was to try and convince her to cut and run with me.

I knocked on her door, already grinning like a fool by the time she threw it open and let me in. She slipped her arms around my neck to pull me into a kiss as she kicked the door shut behind us, and it was like I was finally coming home.

My hands were on her before I could even think to do it, my palms fitting so perfectly into the cinch of her waist it was criminal. Her soft scent was pouring into me and settling warm and heady in my belly, making fire flow through my veins. She made a little sound as I pressed her closer, almost a moan but not quite: part sigh, part hum, but all hunger despite how dainty it was. I slid my hands lower, to her ass, then hauled her up and pressed her back against the wall, keeping a firm hold of her thighs to keep her aloft. Her tongue slid against mine, demanding more from me, and I was helpless but to give her everything I had.

The whole world fell away with her in my arms, my worries about what the fuck I was going to do dissolving into vapor from the heat that was building between us. One of her hands tangled in my hair while the other cupped the nape of my neck, and I wanted to cry from just how fucking *good* that felt. It went deeper than pleasure, more intimate than the feel of her tongue in my mouth or the heat of her sex pressed to my pelvis—it was tender, it was sweet, the way she held me, and it opened up something deep and dark within me, something that lived alongside my nightmares, where my parents died and all the light left the world.

"Eva," I rasped, pressing my forehead against hers as I struggled to get a hold of the terrifying things pouring through me. I had no other words, though—there was just her name, and the questions I refused to speak.

"Sorry," she murmured, kissing the tip of my nose and then pressing her damp kiss-swollen lips to mine again. "I didn't mean to attack you the minute you walked in."

I managed to get a proper breath into my aching lungs. "You mean you didn't invite me over here under false pretenses?" I grinned, ducking my head to trail kisses along the curve of her jaw.

"Mmm..." she hummed, her fingers digging back into my scalp and making me shudder. Veldar's tits, how amazing would this all feel if I wasn't stuck in the damned helix skin—

The sound of a phone ringing cut through the moment, making her stiffen in my arms.

"Shit, that's the work phone. Hold on, I have to go get that."

I let her down, shoving my hands into the pockets of my black leather jacket to hide how they trembled. "Thought you were on lunch, Miss Nadzija. These circumstances are looking more and more suspect..."

"Oh, hush, you. Just give me a sec." She picked up the phone and pressed it to her ear. "Hi there, you've reached Chainlink Insurance and Equities, this is Eva! How can I—oh, hello, yes, sorry, this is her." She was silent for several moments, listening to whoever was on the other end of the call. I had better hearing than most humans, but I couldn't quite make out what they were saying, only that they sounded strained and apologetic.

Whatever it was, it was making Eva's thick brows scrunch tight, the color draining from her face and her mouth dropping open in shock.

"Oh my god," Eva breathed, trembling. I surged forward, clasping her upper arms so I could catch her if she started to fall. "Y-yes, I'll be right there. Give m-me...um, fifteen minutes?" She hung up and immediately dialed another number, ignoring my questions.

"Phil, it's Eva. I'm sorry but there's an emergency I have to go take care of. No, it can't wait. I'm sorry. I know, you'll just have to take it out of my paycheck. Alright. Bye." Then she hung up, her stormcloud eyes wet with tears. I pulled her into my arms, pressing her to my chest.

"What happened?" I asked again, dread making my limbs go numb.

"Maggie, she's hurt. They said—they said some boys at school—"

My heart stopped in my chest. "Where is it?" I asked, grabbing her purse off the table beside us and handing it to her. "Where's the school? I'll drive."

Her delicate pointed chin wobbled, but she pressed her pink lips into a hard line and kept her voice firm when she next spoke. "You don't need to. She's my kid. I can drive—"

"Eva, I'm taking you. Now let's go or I'm slinging you over my shoulder caveman-style and we'll do it that way."

Something in her eyes brightened, those glassy gray orbs widening until I felt like I was going to fall into them. "Why? Why are you doing this?" But despite her question, she followed me when I tugged on her arm.

I didn't really know how to answer her. Something deep inside me was roaring, thumping its fists into its chest and crying out for blood. I didn't know if it was my yvrenii or my felican side, but whatever it was wanted to rip and tear and ruin. It wanted to turn whoever had dared to hurt that beautiful little girl into a smear on the floor. "I care about you. Both of you," I growled as I threw open the door of my little gold sedan and guided her into the passenger seat. "And I want to help in any way I can."

I closed the door on her dazed face, then raced to the other side and started the car. I grabbed Eva's hand and squeezed it tight, and she directed me to Maggie's school in a daze.

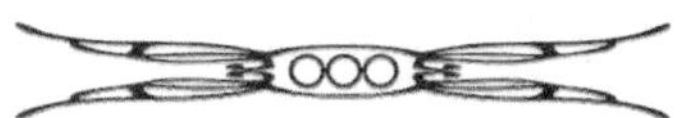

EVA

"I'm so sorry, Ms. Nadya, but there's been an incident. We

need you to come right away. It seems some boys cornered Magdalena in the bathroom and accosted him—er, sorry, her."

I was numb, so beyond fury I could feel nothing. I was trapped in a wrathful daze, the words of the school's guidance counselor—some hack who couldn't even get my child's pronouns or my name right—playing on a mildly distorted loop in my head. I knew I was crying, and shaking, and that Seth was here and he was driving me to the school because he was mad, too, but it was so distant compared to my heart thundering in my chest and calling out for my baby.

It seemed like I blinked and we were there, pulling into the crowded lot and hurrying toward the front entrance. Security met us and escorted me to where everyone was waiting. When they stopped Seth he put a possessive arm around my waist and growled that he was my fiancé, and I didn't bother to correct him. I wanted him there, needed someone else besides me who cared as much for my child as I did, who felt the same outrage and helpless fury that was thrumming through me and making me shake. I could see it in the tense set of Seth's jaw, in the cold steel behind his golden eyes.

When we burst into the room a choked sob escaped my throat as I took in my sweet little girl slumped and ragged in a cheap plastic chair. Those animals had cut all her hair off, leaving it a ragged hacked-off mess, and she had a split lip and several scrapes on her arms and legs. I ran straight to her, ignoring the counselor and principal, ignoring every other two-bit asshole in this room who had failed to do their jobs and protect that which was most precious to me.

I wrapped her up in my arms, clutching her to me as she crumpled in on herself and started crying, clinging to me like she had when she was four and had had a nightmare.

"What the fuck happened?" I heard Seth growl behind me, the low rumble more menacing than if he would have shouted. "Am I mistaken, or are you people supposed to be taking care of these kids and keeping *vrakaash* like this from happening?"

The conversation behind me faded away as I wept and held my crumbling daughter, my heart shattering over and over again in my chest with each distraught sob wracking her thin body. All I could seem to do was chant, over and over again: "It's okay, baby. I'm here. It's okay, I've got you."

A warm hand settled on my shoulder, and then Seth was crouching down beside us, rubbing my back and asking what I needed. I could barely see him through my tears, could barely hear him through the way my heart was crying out at my failure to protect my child from pain. He seemed to understand what I needed anyway though, because he was Seth and he seemed to *always* know. He wrapped both of us up in his arms, and to my eternal shock, it seemed to soothe both of us. Mine and Maggie's tears quieted, the storm dimming as Seth's woodsmoke and leather scent wrapped around us and his warmth seeped into our skin.

Finally calm enough to speak, I stood and stared at the small gathering of people huddled on the far side of the room looking sheepish. Anger flared, chasing away the last of my grief. Seth stood behind me, one hand on Maggie's shoulder and squeezing gently, his hand tattoos on full display. "Where are the cops?" I asked, my voice hoarse and thick with tears. If they'd been called around when I'd been they should be here by now.

"We wanted to wait until you'd gotten here so we could try

and talk this out—"

"*Talk it out*?" I repeated, incredulous. "My daughter has been *assaulted* in your school, on *your* watch, and you think we can just *talk it out*?" I bit back the harsh words clamoring to get out, clenching my jaw hard enough to hurt. "There is *nothing* to discuss here except what you're going to do to the little monsters who did this."

The counselor put her hands up in a placating gesture that just made me more furious. "Ms. Nadya—"

"Nah-JAY-yah," I corrected her.

"Yes, sorry. We understand that you are upset—and rightly so! I can't even imagine what you must be going through right now! But this wasn't a one-sided altercation—"

"Maggie," Seth cut in, and my daughter looked over her shoulder at the absolutely wrathful face of Seth, "Who started it?"

She sniffled, wiping at her nose with a sleeve, and I realized they hadn't offered either of us tissue, so I strode over to the desk and grabbed a wad for each of us from the box perched on the corner. She took it with a watery smile and wiped her face. "They did," she croaked, "they've been fucking with me for months, calling me things because I'm trans, and t-today—" she broke off on a sob, and I tamped down the hurt I felt that this had apparently been going on for months and she'd hid it from me. Now wasn't the time.

"You don't have to go into detail right now, baby," I murmured, smoothing down some of her butchered hair.

"I-I know. I want to." She squared her shoulders and lifted her chin, and she clutched at my hand as she said, "They cornered me in the bathroom. The girl's bathroom. They said I didn't belong in there because I was really a boy and then they held me down and cut off my hair because th-they said it was time to stop pretending—" she swallowed, taking a deep breath. "And then when they let me up I hit them. Kicked them."

I thought I might throw up, I was so disgusted and in shock. "Did you already tell them all that, honey?" I asked my daughter faintly.

She nodded, and I rounded on the assembly of cowering adults watching me like a bomb was about to go off.

Because it was.

"You knew that a hate crime had been committed against a minor on your campus and you *still* didn't think to call the police?" I asked them, fury making my vision go fuzzy. Or maybe it was the fact that I was having trouble breathing that was doing it.

"Calling it a hate crime seems a little extreme, Ms. Nadya —"

"*Nadzija!*" I shouted, my trembling hands curling into tight fists. "My daughter was targeted because of her gender identity, which is *federally protected* according to the Civil Rights Act, making what those boys did a hate crime. They should be expelled and the police should *absolutely* be here!"

"They're on their way, Eva," Seth said from the doorway, snapping me out of my trance. I hadn't even noticed him leave. "Since these idiots didn't feel the need I took it upon myself." He stepped up beside me and pressed a kiss to my temple, so gentle despite the fury evident in every line of his body. "You guys might want to take this time to get your dogs in a row," he added, staring daggers at the school officials. *Did he just say "dogs in a row"?* I had to have misheard him. His presence loosened the mess of knots that had become my chest, letting me breathe easier—though still not easily.

The principal swore, storming off with the guidance counselor in tow. The teacher—who I didn't recognize—gave a pained smile and fled as well, and then we were alone in the small office.

Seth wrapped me in his arms, cradling me against him, and I sighed shakily and let myself sink into him. He was so solid and warm, his scent already so comforting, that I couldn't help but relax, my rage finally cooling to the point I was capable of stringing together real thoughts again. He released me with another chaste kiss, then kneeled in front of Maggie, taking her hands and running his thumbs over the delicate pale skin of her knuckles.

"You okay, Mags?" he asked softly. "No, don't answer that—stupid question. Is there anything I can do?"

She shook her head, pressing her trembling lips into a line. "N-no. Surprise, I guess. I'm trans."

He smiled at her, still holding her hands. "Yeah, that's pretty cool," he told her. "You've got yourself more figured out than a lot of people your age. Shit, you're farther along than *me* in a lot of ways."

Tears tracked down her face. "It doesn't freak you out?" she asked, her voice so small and hesitant I almost crumpled.

Seth snorted, shaking his head. "Not at all. Why would it?"

Maggie lunged forward, wrapping her arms around his neck and sobbing into his shoulder. Seth looked surprised, his eyes wide and his shoulders stiff, before his expression softened and his arms wrapped around her back. He murmured things quietly into her ear as he rocked her, trying his best to comfort her, and as I watched them my last lingering doubts about Seth evaporated.

Something he said made Maggie laugh, and I joined them, smoothing my daughter's hair and rubbing her back alongside Seth. Eventually, she pulled back and I handed her more tissues.

"Once we talk to the police we'll take you to the salon and get your hair fixed up, okay?" I reassured her, feeling wrung out from the powerful emotions that had been coursing through me.

"They didn't give you any ice for that lip?" Seth asked, frowning. Maggie shook her head, and his own lip curled in disgust. "She's not going to keep going here, is she?" he asked me.

"I don't want to just uproot her," I hedged, "but I definitely would rather you went somewhere else." Maggie looked down at her lap, her fingers worrying at the damp tissues.

"That's a lot of extra hassle for you, though," she said quietly. "I'm okay with staying here. Now that it's out in the open those guys—"

"Magdalena," I said, my voice soft but firm. "You have been assaulted here. Do you really think I want you to stay here just to save myself from a little bit of paperwork?" What on Earth was going on here?

"I-it's just—" she gulped and finally looked at me, her expression so miserable I ached. "You've been under so much pressure lately. At work and stuff. I don't want to make things worse for you. You're already having panic attacks and lord even knows what else..."

I stiffened, everything finally clicking into place. The reason she hadn't been telling me about any of this, the reason she was so invested in my seeing Seth, the reason why she was having so much trouble with sleeping and why her style had gotten more and more alt...

She'd been trying to protect me. She'd thought her problems would burden me, that I needed to be shielded from her troubles so I didn't crumple.

How had I failed her so much as a parent?

"Sweetheart, no. Oh my god, *no*. It is *not* your responsibility to protect me. I'm an adult and I can handle this stuff, and when I find myself overwhelmed it is *my* job to get help and figure it out. *Not yours*. You absolutely *do not need* to hide things from me just because I'm stressed out. I need you to tell me these things, Mags." I was crying again, but I couldn't stop it. "Promise me, Maggie: next time you *tell me*. You tell me *right away*. Because no matter what, seeing you hurt is so much worse, I promise you that. Especially knowing what—" the lump in my throat swallowed my words. Knowing what people have done to trans people. How much worse it could have been, when it was already so damn bad.

Seth stood and grabbed us both more tissue just as two uniformed police officers and the principal and counselor from before walked in, looking grim.

The rest of it was a blur, my mind disconnecting itself from everything but the words looping through my head, the grisly pictures of what those animals could have done to my baby flitting through my mind in an unstoppable procession. But I did know that through it all Seth was there, fielding questions, helping me and Maggie with whatever we needed, standing tall and strong and warm behind us, propping us up and keeping us going.

Chapter 10

More Tough Calls

<u>SEPHYR</u>

It felt like someone had ripped my guts out and put them in a blender. Every time I looked at Maggie, at the hacked-off mess of her hair, the streaks of black makeup still clinging to her pale cheeks, the cuts and scrapes peppered over her limbs, I wanted to scream and punch something. She was just a kid trying to live her life; how could people want to do that to her? And how could these *adults* let that happen and then not want to punish the guilty party? My claws had probably torn permanent holes in my palms from just how tightly I was clenching my fists every time the rage swept through me.

I wanted to sweep both of my females up into my arms and carry them away, save them from having to deal with all of this inane *vrakaash*, but it had to get dealt with, so I contented myself with taking on as much of it as I could.

When they'd asked who I was, what my relationship with the Nadzijas was, I lied and said I was Eva's fiancé , a term I'd found which meant that two people were soon to be married, as they called matings. I'd said it because I'd been desperate to stay, to keep close and help all I could, but the longer I thought about it the more...*right* it felt. I kept picturing me and Eva and Maggie all living together, sharing meals, arguing about chores, playing games, watching human movies, and I was filled with so much happiness and light I ached. A part of me felt like they were *mine*, my family, even though I had no right to call them that.

Once the Earth police had gotten the information they needed from us we left, Eva announcing that Maggie would be out the rest of the week. It never occurred to me not to call the police; my females needed their aid, and any negative effects their presence or their questions would have had on me meant nothing in comparison.

I put my arms around their shoulders and guided them out of the school and back out to my car.

Maggie snorted when I unlocked it, swiping at her under eyes once more. "Seth, dude. This car is *so* lame, what the hell are you doing?" Her voice was thick and hoarse but she was smiling, just a little, lifting some of the heavy clouds that had settled over me.

"What would you have expected me to have?" I asked her, sweeping my hand out.

"It should at least be black. Or red. This is a grandma car. As in I *literally* only ever see old women driving it."

I waved my hand dismissively. "Black shows dirt and retains too much heat in the summer. Plus insurance rates are higher on black and red cars. Old Faithful here gets me where I need to go."

Maggie continued her teasing, insisting there had to be a car that was less embarrassing than this one that I could have bought, with Eva tapping at her phone beside me in the passenger seat. During a lull in Maggie's ribbing, she pointed the screen at me, showing search results for a salon nearby.

"Can you drive here, Seth? I think it would be nice to get her hair fixed up before we head home."

"Certainly. You want to go, Mags?" I replied, shooting her a look in the rearview mirror.

"I-I think I would, actually. Thanks, guys."

"Of course, sweetie," Eva reassured her, slotting her phone into my holder so I could follow the directions.

The salon was small and unassuming, part of a chain I saw all over the area. A frazzled-looking stylist rushed over to greet us.

"Hey, hi, welcome," she trilled, tapping at the register's screen. "Do you have an appointment?"

"No," Eva answered, ushering Maggie forward. "My daughter needs her hair fixed up. There was...an event. At school. And they left her with this." Maggie fiddled with the short hanks of hair around her face, flushed and eyes downcast. She'd at least been able to clean off her smeared makeup in the car with some baby wipes I kept in the glove box.

The stylist's face fell, pity filling her wide eyes. "Oh, honey..." she murmured, tapping at the screen in front of her. "María is finishing up with a client right now, but she'll be free to take you after. What's the name?" Eva gave her the necessary information, then we settled into some chairs to wait until Maggie was called over.

Now that we were once more in public Maggie had wilted, folding in on herself and trying to hide in her chair.

"How you doing, Mags?" I asked her gently.

She shrugged, swiping her mangled bangs into her face. "I'm okay," she said, her voice so small and quiet compared to how it usually was.

I frowned, wondering what I could possibly say that would make her feel better. But then a memory popped up that seemed oddly apt. I'd have to obfuscate it with human terminology, but maybe it would be helpful for her to hear it.

"Did you know I'm...biracial?" I asked her.

"Makes sense. I didn't want to assume, though."

I grinned. Maggie was such a good kid; it was *vrakaash* that that had happened to her. "Well, I am. And I grew up in the system, with lots of kids who were hurting and didn't know what to do with it. When I was about ten some of the older kids got ahold of me and shaved me bald." It had been a group of yvrenii kids who hated that I was a "half breed" and part felican. They'd shaved off all of my felican fur, as well as the ginger curls from my scalp, because it was so un-yvrenii to have curly hair. "They took issue with the fact that I had curly hair and the wrong skin color thanks to my mixed heritage and tried to take it away, to erase it from me because something got into their heads thinking they had the right."

I palmed her slim shoulder and squeezed. "But they were wrong. Didn't matter if they got rid of all my hair, or if I swore off all the things that I got from my mother that made me different. I'd still be biracial underneath it all, and no amount of pretending was going to change that."

I ruffled the hair at the back of my head and smiled sheepishly as I realized I was rambling a little. "I'm not so good with words. But do you get what I'm saying?"

She nodded, and Eva took her hand, squeezing it tight.

"I just..." Maggie's eyes darted around, still red from earlier. "I just don't want to look like a boy..." she whispered, cracking my chest open wide.

"You won't," I promised her, my smile feeling a little

shaky. "It's gonna take a lot more than short hair to make a young lady as pretty as you look like a guy."

Almost in sync, my two females got glassy-eyed and I panicked, thinking I'd made it worse. "I'm—" but before I could finish Maggie had thrown herself at me, hugging me tight but letting go just as quickly.

Just then, a smiling young Latina woman rounded the corner, introducing herself as María, and waved Maggie over. Then it was just me and Eva.

"Thank you for saying that," she said, taking the seat Maggie had vacated beside me and grabbing my hand. She leaned her head on my shoulder, and I felt like I was melting at just how sweet the contact was. "I hope this doesn't kick her dysphoria into overdrive. She already struggles with it so much."

"What's that?" I asked, unfamiliar with the term. I kissed the top of her head, breathing in her soft, sweet scent.

"It's like...her brain struggles with the fact that her body doesn't match what her brain sees and it causes distress. Anxiety. Depression. It's very bad and I'm probably describing it poorly."

"Nah, I think I get it." I rested my cheek on her hair, wishing I could stay like this forever and never have to think about Serr'eza and the brotherhood ever again. "Poor kid. I hope she does okay, too. Can we...get fake hair for her? A wig or something?"

"I was going to float the idea by her and see what she thinks," Eva mused. "It's too short and uneven for extensions, I think. And I probably couldn't have afforded them anyway."

"I'm paying for this; whatever it is she needs, I've got it." I needed to do *something* to try and fix this, to bring a smile back to that fierce, protective little cub's face.

Eva started to protest, and I gently covered her mouth with my hand and kissed her forehead. "Nope, I'm not hearing any of that." I tucked in my chin and looked at her sternly. "You will let me do this, Eva. I want to. I have the money." I removed my hand, tracing her bottom lip with my thumb before pulling my hand away entirely. "So you're just going to have to deal with it."

I could see the indecision behind her eyes. She pressed her lips together, then nodded. "Alright. Bossy."

I grinned, throwing my arm around her shoulders and tucking her into my side as best I could despite being on two different chairs. "Yeah, but you like it. If you didn't you wouldn't fold so easily."

She squawked, trying half-heartedly to pull away. "I do *not* need this in my life," she huffed, mirth sparkling in her stormcloud eyes.

That sobered me. No, she did not need this in her life, the absolute shitshow that was Sephyr Kasdaan. She needed someone who could take care of her and Maggie properly, offer them real safety and stability. It didn't matter how badly I wanted to be the male to do it; the sad fact was that I couldn't do that. Not while on the run from Serr'eza and the brotherhood. No matter what I did, at this point anything I did was going to risk my cub and my—

I stiffened as everything clicked into place: Eva was my *mate*. This all-consuming love and obsession I was feeling was the mate bond. Both yvrenii and felicans could develop it, so it was very possible for me to get it despite my mixed heritage.

Instead of filling me with joy, my revelation filled me with cold fear. What was I supposed to do with that information? It just solidified that I was fucked. Even if leaving her would have kept her safe, my body wouldn't let me go far, wouldn't let me stay away from my mate. I'd be drawn to her, sick without her.

But even if—and it was a big fucking "if"—I managed to slip away from Serr'eza with them in tow and make it out alive, it wasn't like I could let things continue this way, living a lie and hiding who I really was. As soon as we got intimate she'd notice something was off; the helix skin could make me look human, but it couldn't do anything about making my body *feel* human, or behave like a human's, and I'd realized early on that I wasn't built like a human man.

Shit, I might have to come clean, I realized.

"Seth?" Eva snapped her fingers in front of my nose, snapping me back into myself. "Where'd you go?"

I shook my head, smiling sheepishly at her. "Sorry, started thinking about work. A uh...a problem just clicked into place." I kissed her cheek. "Sorry."

First thing first: when I got home I needed to use my medbay to check my blood for the markers that signified the development of the mate bond. There was a chance I was wrong, after all.

And from there...Well, I'd just have to figure that out.

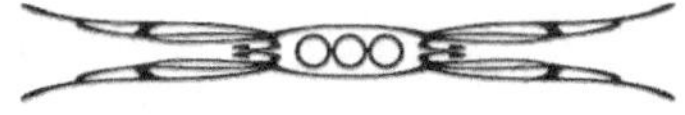

<u>EVA</u>

"You look gorgeous, sweetie," I gushed, admiring Maggie's cute new pixie cut. She still looked unhappy, but I was hopeful.

Seth grinned at her, looking almost...proud? My heart did some very intricate gymnastics routines behind my ribs. How was it that he was so...*good*? I didn't think men were built like him, solid and strong but still gentle and sweet and empathetic.

I could see myself falling for Seth. Especially after today, when he'd dropped everything to help not just me but Maggie, too, treating her carefully but still like *her*, reassuring her and doing his best to make her feel better. And the way he looked at me, the way he touched me...I thought maybe he felt the same. I didn't know how, but despite our age gap, despite the very different paths we'd taken through life to get here, we were falling into something. Something bigger than a chance meeting in a grocery store should've turned into.

Seth tipped the stylist generously, gushing over the magic she'd worked on Maggie's hair, before putting an arm around each of our shoulders and guiding us out to his car. Which...yeah, Maggie was right, it was a very...*elderly-looking* car.

"Where to now, ladies?" He asked as we piled in, flashing us both a grin. Something seemed just the littlest bit off with him, like something was wrong, or bothering him, but he didn't seem upset, per se. Maybe it was just the stress of the day, making me tense and suspicious, or making him feel off.

"Back to my place? I think a day like today calls for oatmeal cookies."

Maggie groaned in anticipation in the backseat. "Oh my gooooooooood Mom, *yes*. Yes please, all the cookies, please. Please Mother, I crave them."

I chuckled, shooting a grin at her over my shoulder. "You got it, kiddo. With chocolate chips?" She nodded. I turned to

Seth, who'd plugged my address into his phone to guide us there. "Well, if you're not busy I hope you'll stay and have some."

"You kidding? I wouldn't miss this for anything. You got everything you need or are we stopping at the store on the way?"

I melted, smiling at him like a loon. "I should have all the ingredients. Thank you though." He reached across the central console and squeezed my knee. I grabbed his hand before he could snatch it back, relaxing into my seat with a sigh. It felt like I'd been running a marathon, I was so drained, my muscles aching from how tightly they'd been clenched since that phone call.

Once we pulled up and filed inside Maggie went to her room to decompress and change out of her dirty clothes, absently patting her shorter hair.

Seth followed me to the kitchen, settling himself at the island counter to keep me company while I worked. I set the oven to preheat, grabbing my bowls and measuring cups from their cabinets along with the ingredients.

I started measuring out my dries to sift together into the bigger bowl. Seth whistled low. "You don't even have to follow a recipe?"

"Nah. I've made these so many times I have it memorized." I met his eyes with a smile. "They're Maggie's favorite, so I tend to make them a lot. Special occasions, pick-me-ups on tough days, incentive to get through chores...really, any excuse will work."

Seth chuckled as he continued to watch me. "How can I help?" he asked, and once again I was struck by just how much he meant it. He wasn't just saying it to be polite, he really meant to help. But I wasn't good at delegating tasks. "It's okay, I've got this. They're really easy."

He frowned, cocking an eyebrow at me. "Fine, but I'm cleaning."

His tone brooked no argument, and I bit my lip at how...*commanding* he sounded. My earlier arousal was starting to trickle back the littlest bit, now that Maggie was home safe. "Yessir," I murmured. His golden eyes darkened, and he leaned toward me, bracing his forearms on the counter.

"Good girl," he murmured, making that spark of arousal flare into a blaze. I sucked in a breath, my eyes locked on his full mouth, curled into a self-satisfied little smile that told me he knew *exactly* what he'd just said. My hands stilled, my task momentarily forgotten, as I licked my lips. His burnished gold eyes shifted to watch my mouth, his cocky grin slipping as something seemed to take hold of him, too.

Then he was pushing back from the counter, standing, walking around to stand beside me, until he could pull me close and kiss me senseless. His hands wrapped around my waist, settling on my hip and the small of my back and guiding me closer to the heat pouring off of him. I wrapped my arms around his neck, and then he was leaning close, slanting his mouth over mine in a slow, sultry press that lit me on fire. He moaned into my mouth, his tongue gliding against mine like I was the most delicious thing he'd ever tasted. His fingers dug into my flesh, his nails surprisingly sharp and managing to prick my skin, but it only wound me tighter, making me clutch at him with something approaching desperation.

What was it about Seth that felt so *right*? Why was it that my body was waking up for him when I'd barely felt anything like desire for years? Why him? Why now?

And why was I so hellbent on questioning it?

In defiance of the little voice in my head that was determined to be a buzzkill, I arched my back and pressed my breasts into his chest, moaning at the delicious friction from just that little bit of contact. One of his hands slid down to cup my ass, broad fingers digging into my soft flesh and hefting it, squeezing it, urging me closer still so that I could feel the hard bar of his erection pressing into my hip. Electricity and heat shot through me in a wave that took my breath away, making me melt into his leather and woodsmoke scent.

"Jesus christ, get a room, you pervs."

I ripped myself away from Seth, my face hot and throbbing with shame. I couldn't even look at Seth, I was so embarrassed about being caught getting handsy by my fourteen-year-old daughter.

"We're adults, we can play grabass in the kitchen if we want," Seth drawled smoothly, crossing his arms over his chest and smirking.

Maggie pursed her lips together and tried to glare but wound up giggling instead. Was this inappropriate? She was getting older and would undoubtedly be curious about sex and affection, and we'd both been fully clothed.

"Sorry you had to see that, dear," I told her as I turned back to the half-finished cookie dough, "but maybe the next time you'll announce yourself properly," I teased.

She snorted, grabbing a glass from the cabinet and filling it with ice water. "What, like in medieval times, where kings had those guys with trumpets going in and announcing them?"

I nodded. "Exactly like that. We don't really have the budget for that so you'll have to do it all yourself but it's either start being a herald or get used to walking in on me getting smooched."

"I think I still have my recorder from third grade," Maggie supplied thoughtfully, taking the seat beside Seth at the counter.

"Is that a threat?" Seth asked with one of his signature grins.

"Oh yeah," Maggie responded, taking a big gulp of her water.

He elbowed her gently. "Your hair looks good, kid. Very Audrey Hepburn."

Her smile faded a touch, and she combed through it with her fingers self-consciously. "You don't...you don't think it makes me look like a boy?"

Seth snorted. "Not in the slightest. You're a girl, it's your hair, so how could it? I mean there's tons of guys with long hair and that doesn't suddenly make them girls, right?" He sat back in his chair with a shrug. "Anyone who thinks gender has anything to do with hair is a fucking idiot and you should laugh in their faces."

Maggie smiled softly. "Trust me, I would," she said, sneaking a handful of chocolate chips from the bag before I could snatch it from her. "Don't want to get beat up, though," she finished around her mouthful of chocolate.

"I can teach you some moves," Seth offered. "Had to learn how to handle myself when I was young, and now it's kind of my job to kick ass."

Her eyes lit up. "Really?"

"Oh yeah, absolutely. First lesson: if you're smaller than your opponent then you gotta try and use your body weight against them. Even if they're twice your size, having to deal with all hundred-plus pounds of you at once is probably going to throw them unless they're an actual pro. You know what all the vulnerable spots are to go for?"

I wanted to interject and say this wasn't an appropriate conversation, that I didn't want to encourage Maggie to be violent, but hadn't today proved she needed to be able to defend herself? That she couldn't always rely on the people around her to keep her safe?

These were the things that were truly difficult about raising a child—the moments that were full of doubt and uncertainty, the moments where you worried that you were doing something terribly wrong, that this would be the moment where you ruined them or their life forever.

In the end, I let Seth give her a self-defense lecture while I finished up the cookies and got them in the oven.

In a weird way, once I'd relaxed into the moment it felt unnervingly domestic. It shouldn't have—my boyfriend (if that was what he even was to me) was sitting there teaching my recently attacked daughter some basic self-defense facts while I hummed away, baking the edge off of my nerves. But the fact was that it *did* feel homey, and right, made me think that I really could let Seth into mine and Maggie's lives. We'd just met him, but the guy was fitting in so smoothly, like he'd always been meant to be here.

Soon the smells of chocolate and sugar and warm butter were wrapping around us like a blanket, chasing away the chills of what had happened and letting me finally relax the rest of the way. I looked at Maggie and took my first full breath in hours. *She's okay. She's fine. She's right here*, I told myself.

"Holy shit, those smell amazing," she groaned, surging to her feet and trying to see into the dark oven without moving around to the other side of the island. "Can I just dip in there real quick and snatch one?"

I shook my head. We had this conversation every time. "Four more minutes. Your obsession with raw dough is going to land you in the hospital one of these days, monkey."

"But the danger is what makes it taste so *good*!" she whined, sitting back down with a pout.

"What's wrong with eating raw dough?" Seth asked, looking genuinely puzzled.

"You might get salmonella from the raw egg. It's a nasty bacteria, it can kill you." Had no one ever told him that? Jeez, he really *had* had a hard life.

His eyes widened, one hand combing back through his copper curls. "Seriously? And you still eat eggs? Like, all the time?"

I laughed. "Not *raw*! We cook them and they're fine. Heat kills any salmonella that might be on there." The alarm I'd set on my phone went off, and I turned to check the cookies and see if they were done.

Satisfied that they were sufficiently golden brown, I pulled them from the oven and set the cookie sheet on the stove burners for them to cool. Maggie, of course, swooped in and took two of the still-molten baked goods and threw them back without any hesitation. Her mouth dropped open, giving me a clear view of her chewed-up food, and I laughed as she alternated between panting and making noises of delight.

"Did you burn your tongue?" I asked after she'd

swallowed.

"Oh yeah, big time," she declared, proudly shoving in the next one.

I shook my head, laughing despite myself. Of all the things to have an unhealthy addiction to, eating cookies when they were too fresh from the oven wasn't one of the ones I was worried about.

I got my smallest plates out of the cabinet and dished out two for each of us, setting them down on the island, where there was more room than our table. "Give them a couple of minutes to cool," I told Seth. "Unless you're also a maniac who doesn't care about burning your mouth like my daughter."

"It helps my tongue peel," she insisted with a straight face.

"Tongues are not supposed to peel, baby. Please tell me you're kidding."

"Maaaaybe." Maggie took a cookie from the plate I'd handed her and shoved it in her mouth. "Om nom nom, delicious tongue peel," she said in a Cookie Monster voice.

I rolled my eyes and picked up one of my own treats, blowing on it delicately before taking a small nibbling bite. It was still a little too hot for me, but there really was something magical about biting into a fresh baked good, the heavenly scent of its cooking still hanging heavy and sweet in the air.

"What do you think, Seth?" Maggie asked, and I looked over at him.

He was just sitting there looking shocked and vaguely upset. "Seth?" I called softly. "Are you okay, hun?"

He blinked, drawing in a deep shuddering breath before he turned too-bright eyes on me. "I have no words, Eva," he breathed.

"Oh shit, you made him have a religious experience,"

Maggie giggled.

A dazed smile cracked across his face. "You laugh, but she absolutely did," he said quietly, still looking at me like I'd shown him his god. "This is the most delicious thing I've ever had." He took another bite, closing his eyes in bliss and moaning so deeply I felt it in my core. "It reminds me of my parents, somehow. They died when I was four, and I thought I only—that I didn't remember anything about them. But I remember something when I taste these."

Jesus, had my silly little cookies really done that? "What do you remember?" I asked him quietly, reaching across the island for his hand. He took it, rubbing his thumb over my knuckles idly.

"I came into the kitchen to ask for a drink because I was thirsty. But when I walked in I saw my dad twirling my mom around in his arms, both of them laughing about something. When he stopped spinning he leaned down and kissed her, and then I went back to my room to play because I didn't want to interrupt them." He swallowed, tears turning his gold eyes molten. "Something that smelled like these had been cooking, I think."

I looked at Maggie, who was looking between me and Seth with an expression I couldn't quite read. I dropped his hand and came around to stand beside him, wrapping him up in my arms and pulling his face into my chest. He clung to me, not crying but very close, very clearly overwhelmed. After a moment Maggie came closer and joined the hug, her hands winding up on my waist.

Seth made a strangled noise deep in his throat, then he freed one of his arms to put it around Maggie's shoulders.

So much had happened today, so much of it bad, and it

was soothing on a level I couldn't fully comprehend to just stand there with them, the warmth of the kitchen mingling with the warmth pouring through my chest, with the ache in my heart that told me it was too late to stop myself from falling for Seth.

Chapter 11

Seph Makes His Debut

<u>SEPHYR</u>

I didn't really have to do the bloodwork when I got home —there was no doubt in my mind now that this female was my mate, that this child was meant to be my child. That the two of them were the family I hadn't even known I was searching for ever since I was just a cub.

So what the fuck was I going to do?

Once I'd gotten ahold of myself and ended the hug we finished our food in comfortable silence.

"It's criminal that you aren't sharing these things with the world," I told her as I stood at the sink cleaning up. I'd had to practically tie her to the chair to let me do it. "You are incredibly talented and could absolutely go pro."

Eva was smiling sadly when I glanced over my shoulder at her. "You know why, babe. Even if I can get a loan it'll be a long time, probably years, before I can turn a profit big enough to live off of. Maybe once Maggie's in college I can try doing a small side thing on the internet or something."

I frowned down at the sudsy mixing bowl in my hands. "I could help you. To get it going now." I had stolen enough money to stay undercover for years; why shouldn't I give it to Eva to follow her dreams?

I'd give her the bleeding heart straight from my chest if she asked for it.

"I couldn't do that to you, Seth. You just met me. And I don't know if I'd be able to pay you back anytime soon—"

"Perfect, because it would be a gift anyway," I told her.

I finished rinsing the bowl and turned off the water, the dishes all clean now that that was done. I dried off my hands and sat beside her, taking her hands. "Didn't you say all the best things in life are risky? Let me help you take this risk and make it a little less…risky." *Damn, do I ever have a way with words,* I thought sarcastically.

She blinked at me, her brow furrowed. "But…but who will take care of Maggie if I'm busy with a new business?"

I shrugged. "I could help with that, too. I used to tutor some of the younger kids in the foster homes I got placed in. I'm rusty but I bet I could help with that, and driving her around and cooking and stuff." I captured her chin and tilted her face to look me dead in the eyes so she could see how serious I was. "I can do it. I *want* to do it."

She bit her lip, drawing my eye to those soft pink petals. "But why? *Why* are you doing all of this for us?"

I swallowed. "Honestly?…I don't know. I can't really explain it, but I feel…drawn to you. To protect and care for you and make you happy anyway I can." I swallowed, searching her gray eyes. "I've never felt this before, but as much as it scares me it also feels so damn *right*."

She searched my face for several long seconds, my lungs refusing to fill until she said something to me. I was so scared, now that the words were out. What if she rejected me? What if she didn't want me? What if I'd freaked her out and she wanted nothing else to do with me?

She smiled softly, getting to her feet and tugging me along with her by the hand. She led me through her small house, not saying anything and making me more panicky by the second.

I hadn't been this scared in ages.

Finally, we got to a room that looked like it was probably her bedroom. On the other end of the hall was a closed door that was clearly Maggie's room, the door closed because she'd announced she'd needed a nap once she'd eaten. A bathroom and closet separated the two bedrooms. She closed and locked the door behind us, then led me over to her bed, carefully made with a pretty galaxy pattern on the blanket and sheets. I wanted to laugh: my mate was interested in the stars. Would she want to go to space with me? To see the stars and visit other worlds?

Would she still care for me even after seeing how I really looked?

Once we were both seated she turned to me, angling her body to face me and bringing a knee up onto the bed so she wouldn't have to twist uncomfortably. I mirrored her, scooting close enough that our knees touched. Then she cupped my face in her hands and slanted her mouth over mine, kissing me softly and sweetly.

I felt like I might cry all over again. My hands were on her, clinging to her with frantic desperation, like I could stop the forces threatening to tear us apart if I could just hold on to her tight enough.

It didn't take long for our kiss to turn searing, Eva climbing into my lap and running her hands over my chest, running her thumbs over my nipples and making my cock so hard it ached all up and down my legs.

"I want you," she gasped into my mouth, her hips grinding into me and driving me wild.

Fuck, I wanted her more than anything. But I couldn't in good conscience have sex with her without her knowing the whole truth.

But I could still make her feel good.

With a growl that was all yvrenii, I hoisted her up and turned us so she was flat on her back on the bed. "Don't got protection," I told her as I slid one of my hands down her body until my palm was pressing into her mound through her jeans. "But I'd like to take care of you, if that's alright."

Eva froze, her eyes going wide and uncertain. "L-like...like oral?" I nodded. She bit her lip, looking pained. "Um...I have something I need to talk to you about before we...do that."

She was incredibly nervous, which got me worried, but how bad could it be? "Sure, what is it?"

Her fingers twisted into the fabric of her shirt, And she pressed her lips together into a line so tight they flashed white.

"I-I have this skin thing. It looks nasty, but I promise y-you can't catch it. It's autoimmune. S-so like, um, it's kind of genetic. Or something like that." Her eyes slipped from mine and she tried to turn her face away, to hide from me, but even though I was hiding so much from her, I was a hypocrite and couldn't let her do that; I grabbed her chin and urged her to look back at me.

"I promise you I won't care," I told her, meaning every inch of it. She could have a portal to a hell dimension embedded in her belly button with a mess of tentacles wriggling through trying to kill me and it would barely make me pause. I was too far gone for this woman, my mate.

She swallowed and her stormcloud eyes went pleading. "It's mostly in remission these days but I do still get the occasional active site and—it's so *bad*, Seth. Gorey. And the scars..."

I dipped my head and kissed her trembling lips, cupping the side of her face and rubbing her cheekbone with my thumb. "Everybody's got scars, sweetness," I told her when I broke the kiss. "Yours aren't going to bother me. But if it's too much..."

She considered, searching my face, and I wished I could see her with all three of my eyes. In yvrenii mythology, the third eye was to see the truth of the world, and being able to behold one's mate with it was a holy gift. The urge to reveal myself, to let her see the whole of me, was almost overwhelming. She was being so brave, putting this vulnerable part of herself out there, and here I was steeped in lies and illusions, denying my mate the honesty she was owed.

Something in her gaze hardened, becoming sure. "No, I want you to see. If it's going to scare you off it's better to know now."

"Won't scare me off, you lunatic," I teased, kissing her again. "But thank you. For trusting me with this. With everything." It wasn't even the least I could do, to show her how much she meant to me, but it was something.

My hand slid back down her body, joining hers where she was fiddling with the closure of her pants. I helped her strip off her jeans, leaving her in her simple cotton briefs. Her very *damp* briefs that clung to the shape of her pussy and made my mouth water.

Even in just her panties, I could see what she was talking

about: the skin on her inner thighs and the crease where her legs met her pelvis was darkened and twisted with countless scars. Most were purple or red and looked painful, even though they were probably long since healed.

She was avoiding looking at me, her eyes trained on a corner of the ceiling. I leaned down and kissed her, trying to pour everything I was feeling into it. "You're beautiful," I promised her, leaning my forehead against hers. It pressed strangely on my third eye, but it also felt right.

I kissed her one more time then buried my face in the crook of her neck and breathed her sweet scent in deep. Nuzzling and nipping at her jawline and throat, my fingers started on the buttons of her blouse, wanting to see more of her, to feel more of her and show her how much I loved every inch of this skin that she was so ashamed of.

I slid a little further down her body, pressing kisses along her collarbone until I got to the hollow of her throat, gradually creeping lower until I was nuzzling at the satiny skin on the tops of her breasts. "This still okay, gorgeous?" I asked, my index finger tracing the silky-soft valley between the quivering mounds.

"Yes, it is very much okay," she responded breathlessly, arching up into my touch. I grinned, then slid the cups of her bra down to expose her perfect tits.

She had a couple of other scars peeking out from the bottom of the bra band, I realized, and even in her armpits. They looked like they hurt, and I wished I could somehow take that pain away from her. I dipped my head, pressing kisses to some of the scars before I turned my attention to the rosy-brown peaks of her nipples and sucked one into my mouth.

She gasped, her hands cradling my head, her fingers digging into my scalp and making my cock throb harder in my pants. I could feel my sleeve dripping, it was so ready and wet, and I wanted nothing more than to shred the rest of her clothes and join my body with hers as the yvrenii god Veldar had intended.

But if I took from her like that, knowing I was holding back so much, I'd feel like a monster. So instead I took my pleasure from hers, from figuring out what touches got me more of her gasps and breathy moans.

Once I'd lavished both breasts with attention she was panting and writhing beneath me, and I knew I couldn't wait any longer—I had to taste her. I had to make her come all over my face more than I needed my next breath.

I released her nipple with a pop, then kissed further down her body, licking the silvery marks on her belly no doubt left over from when she carried Maggie, until I was at the waistband of her panties.

"Can I take these off?" I asked her, my voice so rough and gravelly I didn't recognize it.

She tried to remove them herself, but I swatted her hands away and hooked my thumbs into them and pulled them down and off, with Eva lifting her hips and wriggling to help things along.

"There you are," I purred, spreading her thighs with my hands and settling between them. I could feel the tension creeping back into the muscles under my palms as self-consciousness started to take hold, but I wasn't put off by the scars in the slightest. I was glad she'd warned me, because otherwise I would have been concerned she was hurting, but she was still the most gorgeous thing I'd ever seen, and I made sure to tell her that. "You're so perfect, *pra'ja*," I murmured, the felican term of endearment for a mate falling from my lips so easily. "Told you it wouldn't bother me."

She let out a breathy chuckle, her fingers just brushing the side of my face. "Should have known you'd love being right too much to be both—*oh god*!" I silenced her sass by spreading her wide and licking down the wet seam of her.

Human women weren't built too differently from felican women, but she was fairly different from the one yvrenii female I'd been with. But I knew from my research on human sexuality that the half-hidden bud of flesh at her apex was where I'd want to focus my attention.

I dove in, swirling my tongue in firm circles, adjusting my angle as I chased after the spots that would drive her wild.

It wasn't long before I found a rhythm that seemed to be working, Eva writhing and panting and whimpering beneath me. She ground her hips into my mouth, her fingers digging into my hair, tugging on it and spurring me on. She was chanting under her breath, choking back moans so Maggie wouldn't hear her, but it seemed like she needed more.

I teased at her entrance with my fingers, dipping them into her quivering channel and crooking my finger to try and find the spot I'd read about. I knew I'd found it when she froze, going dead silent, so I honed in on that spot, then closed my lips around her clit and sucked it gently into my mouth.

She snatched a pillow from behind her and smashed it into her face to stifle her screams as she came *hard*. Her inner walls and clit were fluttering and throbbing around me, moisture coating my hand as she shook and shook. I should let up, give her breathing room, but I wanted to wring her dry, force her body to give me everything it had.

I didn't let up until she pushed me off of her, complaining about being too sensitive.

I sat up on my elbow, licking my hand clean and then wiping my face, only to lick my hand again.

Eva, already flushed from her orgasm, squeaked and hid her face again. "Do you have to be so lewd?" she asked, her voice muffled.

I snorted, kissing the delicate skin of her inner thigh.

"I haven't even begun to be lewd, my dear," I told her.

EVA

I...okay. Whoa. That was...wow

Yep, I was definitely going to have to marry Seth. I mean, after getting head like that my hands were basically tied.

But just as important as the unbelievable orgasm was that he'd seen all my scars and he hadn't flinched in the slightest. He'd dived right in like they were nothing to him. Maybe they even *were* nothing to him.

Once the atoms of my brain managed to re-conglomerate and give me some thoughts to think I struggled upright and reached for his belt. "Your turn, now."

But he took my hand from his pants and kissed my knuckles delicately. "Naw, this was all about you, babygirl," he told me, shooting me one of his cocky self-satisfied little smirks. "I'm good."

I cocked an eyebrow at him. "I mean, yes you are quite good at that," I allowed, making his smile lighten into something more soft and joyful, "but I didn't think it was possible for a guy to turn down oral. What are you, some sort of alien or something?"

All amusement fled Seth's face, his eyes going wide and uncharacteristically panicked. He gulped and sat up, taking my hands in his. "Yes," he breathed, squeezing my fingers with clammy hands. "I am."

I drew back, frowning in confusion. "This is a weird time for a joke."

He licked his lips, eyes darting down to my naked body. "You should get dressed. And get Maggie. I'm an alien and I want to tell you everything."

I yanked my hands from his grasp, unease settling over me like a cowl. *See, this is why you don't date*, I scolded myself. *There's always a catch, and more often than not they're crazy.* "You're scaring me, Seth. This isn't funny." I fixed my bra and slid off the bed, swapping my work clothes for some comfy sweats as fast as I could. Once I was dressed I turned back to him, now standing beside the foot of the bed and wringing his hands.

"I-I don't want to lie to you anymore, Eva. I think—I think I'm falling for you and I don't want to keep anything from you. But what I've got to say..." He swiped trembling hands over his face, pleading with me with those unusual golden eyes of his. "You're going to hate me when I'm done with it, but I just...I have to tell you."

I crossed my arms over my chest, pressing my lips into a firm line to stop them from trembling. "I think I'd like for you to leave now," I whispered, too frightened to speak any louder. "Please."

"Eva..." Seth said, taking a step towards me. I backed up until my butt hit my dresser behind me.

He sagged, his eyes filling with so much pain I almost felt bad. But I lifted my chin and held firm. He nodded, looking away, before getting a strange look on his face that made me tense up.

After a few seconds, his skin shimmered like a mirage, making me start and knock a picture over on the top of the dresser, and then between one blink and the next Seth was...different. Transformed.

Possibly what was the most strange was the fact that he still looked so much like himself. It was the same tawny skin and copper curls, but there was some fur on his forearms and peeking out of his shirt collar now. It was still his golden eyes looking at me with so much fear and pain, but there was a third smaller one above and between them. Those were still his broad, strong hands but they were tipped with sharp claws instead of nails. He bit his same full lips, but I caught a glimpse of fangs and tiny tusks on his bottom jaw.

"My real name is Sephyr Kasdaan," he said softly, begging me with his eyes to not run, to hear him out. "I'm from a planet in the Gathus sector called Exodia and I'm a mercenary who came here on a job. One that I never had any intention of doing, because really I'm gonna run and hide here on Earth from the guys who hired me. And I—I want you and Maggie to come with me when I go to ground."

I opened my mouth to say something, to respond to Seth —no, *Sephyr*—in a calm and rational way that would allow us to discuss this new development like adults. But all that came out was a blood-curdling shriek that made him wince—and made two little catlike ears peeking out of the top of his hair twitch. I didn't know why, but the sight of that was what made my knees buckle, and not even my grip on the dresser kept me from sliding to the floor.

There was a bang from down the hall, and then Maggie was bursting into the room, her old softball bat cocked and ready to swing. "Mom!" she called, running to me and getting in between me and Sephyr.

And that was when she noticed him. "S-Seth?"

He smiled grimly. "Hey, kiddo. Surprise."

The bat clattered to the floor. "What the fuck, man?" she breathed.

"I was just uh...clearing the air. To recap: I'm an alien. My name is actually Sephyr Kasdaan. I'm a terrible person who lied to you both and I will see myself out." He turned to leave, but Maggie surged forward, grabbing his forearm.

"No, wait!" she said. "Why are you leaving?"

He cocked his head to the side, then swept his free hand over his newly revealed alien form.

"Are you going to hurt us?" Maggie asked as I got to my feet.

Sephyr shook his head. "Never. I'd *never* hurt you." His eyes darted to me, full of pleading earnestness. "Either of you."

"Good. Then don't go. We...we'll talk about this. Right, Mom?" Maggie turned to me, and I found myself nodding, stuck in a daze that might have been shock.

Of all the things I might have expected, my boyfriend revealing he was from another planet was low on the list, but if I was being honest with myself, it didn't surprise me too terribly; I mean, since when did human men *get* me and find me attractive? Even Maggie's dad hadn't actually been interested in me. He'd made it very clear my having HS freaked him out, and that he didn't really believe me when I said it wasn't an STI.

I was a little hurt, beneath the shock, but at the same time I couldn't exactly blame the guy for hiding the fact that he was an alien. As far as anyone on Earth knew, aliens were as much of a fairy tale as unicorns or dragons, and if he'd studied us well enough to pass then he definitely knew that we were unkind to what was new and unknown.

"L-let's go in the living room," I said weakly, wanting to be able to get into a larger space and feel like I could breathe again. Somehow I'd avoided a panic attack up until now, but I was rapidly approaching my limit.

Sephyr nodded, and Maggie dropped his arm, letting him take his leave while I got my feet under me. I watched his back as he slipped down the hall, and a hysterical laugh bubbled up my throat that I barely managed to choke off when I saw the littlest stub of a tail, like a manx cat, twitching above the waistband of his pants. Maggie heard my little snicker and gently elbowed me in the side. "Don't be rude, Mom," she hissed, barely controlled amusement tightening her own mouth.

"You two better not be laughing at my tail," Sephyr called from the living room around the corner from where were in the hallway, making us both burst out into laughter that was only a *little* hysterical.

He was sitting all by himself in the only armchair, his arms crossed over his chest and looking supremely uncomfortable. His leg jumped wildly, and he looked wary, like he fully expected us to attack him.

It was then that I remembered that he'd said often that he'd had a rough life, that he'd had a lot of painful things happen to him, and that he might fully expect us to hurt him, to flay him alive and do our worst.

I'd be lying if I said I didn't want to; a very small part of me was furious and calling for blood, wanting retribution for being deceived and lied to, for being made to feel foolish. But I sat on the loveseat beside Maggie and took her hand, the two of us facing the man who had taken such good care of us that I knew I at least owed him a chance to explain.

"So..." I began, biting my lip and feeling awkward and sorely out of my depth. "You're not from around here. That's...interesting. Um—so—"

"How much of what you told us was true?" Maggie interjected, saving me from embarrassing myself further.

Sephyr licked his lips, squirming a little in his seat. "The broad strokes stuff. About me and my life. I should have lied *more*, to be honest. Normally I would but with you..." he was looking right at me now, the eye contact so intense I almost couldn't handle it. "With you, I couldn't do it. I only fudged the details that would have outed me as not human." His eyes dropped, the third one closing entirely. "I know you have no reason to believe me, but I'm telling the truth. You two know more about me than anyone else has known for a while. Maybe ever. Even with...all this."

I snorted. Sephyr's eyes snapped to me, and a slow grin spread on his face. It may have been sharper, more toothy, but it was the same cocky grin I'd grown addicted to at its core. It relaxed something in me, to see it. "What's so funny?" he asked me, nothing but amused curiosity in the question.

"I don't know, honestly. I guess I just found it kind of cosmically funny that you decided the people you were trying to dupe the hardest were the people you opened up to the most."

He chuckled, still grinning at me. "You see, that's what I love about you, Eva: you're always finding the humor in things." He uncrossed his arms, lowering his hands into his lap and clasping them together tight, his leg still juddering wildly with his nerves. His two parallel eyes dropped to the floor, but his third slid over to my face as he asked, "Do you hate me for this?"

It was the quietest, most vulnerable question I'd ever heard from any guy ever, and it compelled me to get up from my seat to crouch down in front of him, my knee popping loudly when I did. "No," I told him, grabbing one of his clawed hands. The back was softly furred, like very hairy men sometimes got, but despite those little differences it was still Seth's huge warm hand I was holding, and that helped my brain start merging the two. His woodsmoke smell wrapped around me, and I met his closed-off golden eyes as I repeated, "No. I don't think I hate you. It's just a lot to process, you know? Not only are aliens real, but it turns out my boyfriend is one."

He smiled at me hesitantly. "So I'm your boyfriend, then?"

I snorted. "Only taking in the most important information, I see." I squeezed his hand. "Yeah, dummy. Of course you are. After today how could you not be? What you've done for me, for Maggie...that's not casual, Sephyr—"

"You can call me Seph," he interjected softly.

"Seph," I agreed, testing it out. It was funny that even his fake name had been so close to reality. "It's not casual. I don't...I don't just let people into my life like this. So if you're willing to give me some time to fit this information into my brain then I think we can work this out."

He smiled at me, hope making his eyes pour warmth, but

after a moment his look soured, his eyes closing off and avoiding mine.

"See, that's the thing," he told me, clutching at my hand tight, as if he was afraid I'd run and he meant to stop me.

I swallowed, getting to my feet with a soft groan. I sat on the arm of the chair, staying close because something told me he needed me for this. "What is it, Seph?"

"Yeah, rip it off like a bandaid," Maggie cut in, watching us.

He sighed, pressing his lips together hard enough they flashed white. His grip on my hand grew tighter, more desperate. "When I told you I was mixed up in some bad shit...I wasn't lying. I'm less mixed up in the worst things than I used to be, but I'm still a mercenary. And a few months ago I got an offer from some real bad guys I owed money to. The job was absolutely disgusting, but I took it anyway because I wanted out. I wanted a fresh start and coming somewhere like Earth, where I could just disappear..." His hand had gone sweaty in mine, but I didn't let go. Tension thrummed through every inch of his compact body.

"Serr'eza and the th'rak brotherhood...they're ruthless. Don't give a shit about the wider universe, about anyone but themselves." Seph let go of my hand and leaned forward, bracing his elbows on his thighs and cradling his head in his hands. "He's threatened to kill me if I don't deliver. And even if he doesn't murder me I owe him so many credits I have no hope of paying away my debt. So I have three more days to disappear. I'll have to leave Chicago, possibly the United States entirely. I'll have to go off the grid, destroy all my tech...and I know it's so much to ask but...I want you to come with me. Both of you."

Seph went silent, and I stepped back, returning to the loveseat with Maggie so I could clutch her tight. "Go...go where?"

He shrugged, looking anguished. "I haven't gotten that far yet. But I have a forged passport and can whip a couple up for you, if you'll go with me."

I shook my head, my brow lowering over my eyes. "But my job...Maggie's education...what would be live off of?"

Seph's head dropped, his shoulders slumped in defeat. "I...stole a lot of money when I came here. *Vrakaash*, I know it's a lot to ask, Eva. That I have no right to ask it. But..."

I didn't know what to say. I'd never considered leaving Chicago, let alone the US, and now here was Seph asking me to trust him—having lied to me from the start about who and what he was—and let him take us god only knew where?

"No," Maggie said quietly, her voice thick with tears and pain. "We can't—Mom, we have to go with him." Seph's three eyes snapped to her face and he gave her a sad smile. "Or—or we can fight them! I bet—" I put my hand on Maggie's shoulder and squeezed, urging her to silence.

"I wish I could wipe that scum off the face of the universe, but I'm out-gunned, Mags. Even with a fierce warrior like you backing me up." Maggie sniffled, clutching at my hand on her shoulder. "And the person coming for me...he doesn't care about hurting a cub or an innocent woman." He looked at us with glassy eyes. "I won't risk you two," he insisted, voice firm. "And...fuck, I am *so sorry*. But there's a small chance that no matter how careful I was, Siit'ron or whoever gets sent after me will discover my connection to you. So coming with me... might be the only choice. For us all to hide and hope the Collective doesn't come calling for me."

"Is that…your police? Your government?" I asked quietly.

He nodded. "The enforcers are like the police, yeah. There's a ship of theirs that's been in orbit since I got here. I'm not sure why, but it could be bad." He licked his lips, all three eyes pleading with us, though I wasn't sure why anymore.

"Before, in the kitchen…you said you'd help us. That you'd take care of Maggie and support me while I follow my dreams." I searched his face, holding his anguished gaze. "Could we still do that? Is there…enough?"

He blinked, brows furrowing. "Um…yeah, I don't see why not. Are you saying—"

I smiled at him, then looked at my daughter quietly crying beside me. She nodded, leaning her head on my shoulder. "We'll do it. We'll come with you." I licked my dry lips, tears gathering. "I—I love you. Of course we're going with."

"You don't mean that," he rasped. My eyes were too clouded by tears to see his expression, but he sounded like I'd just stabbed him.

"Like hell I don't," I sniffled, aching with how true it was, that I'd somehow managed to start falling for this maniac after a couple of weeks. But the fact of the matter was that despite the mountain of shit I'd just learned, I still couldn't imagine my life without him. He just fit so perfectly into my little family, into the cracks of myself that I hadn't even realized were there.

"Come here," I croaked, holding out the arm opposite the one I held Maggie with.

He hesitated, sitting too still and tense in the armchair, but then he surged to his feet with a growl and crouched to scoop us both into his arms. Warmth and woodsmoke wrapped around me and it was so beautiful, so *right* that a sob escaped my throat. "This is right," I whispered, burying my face into his throat. "This needs to stay."

Seph let out a choked laugh. "Yeah, I think so too," he rasped as he kissed my hair.

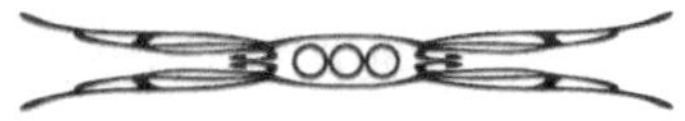

<u>SEPHYR</u>

I didn't know what I'd done to deserve someone like Eva, but I was determined to keep her for as long as she'd let me. "This is right," she'd said as I'd pulled her and Maggie into my embrace, and I didn't think anyone had ever said something so true before in all of Veldar's creation.

Suddenly, Maggie let out a gasp and pulled back. "Witness protection!" she cried, jumping to her feet and running for her room.

I stood, trying to return to my seat, but Eva tugged me down beside her, her much smaller hand clutching at mine and making my heart clench in my chest. I wanted to kiss her, but thought it best if I held off until she made that move.

Maggie returned with her phone clutched in her hand, screen pointed towards us. "Cut a deal with the space cops! Turn in the asshole and all his cronies but make sure they give you immunity and shit."

I blinked, surprised. It went against every single one of my criminal instincts, but it did make a certain kind of sense. I was out-gunned taking on the brotherhood all by myself, but against the Collective they'd be no match. "That's not a bad idea, Mags," I said slowly. "But I don't know if they do stuff like that..." At least, *I'd* never heard of it.

But there were certain protections in place for mated pairs, since forced separation was considered psychological torture for those species for whom the bond existed. And as a primitive species, humans were doubly protected. Which meant that no matter what, Maggie and Eva would be alright even if I threw myself on the mercy of the Collective and they locked me up instead.

I finally looked at Maggie's phone, which was opened up to what looked like an encyclopedia page about a human thing called the Witness Protection Program. I skimmed the article, seeing why she'd thought it would be a good idea. "I can certainly try something like this," I said slowly, pushing at her phone to let her know I was done looking at it. "I can imagine that the Collective would appreciate intel on this particular chapter of the brotherhood. They're one of the more prolific in the slavery market." I twisted my mouth to the side, hating to quash the hope shining out from their beautiful faces. "But I still think running is the best option."

"But you just said those guys are evil, that they're slavers —" Maggie gasped, her fingers pressing into her mouth. "Do they enslave *humans?*"

I nodded, my face grim. "Yeah. They've been coming here for longer than I've been alive. Taking people and…selling them."

Both Eva and Maggie had gone pale. "Then even if we get away, they'll just keep doing this. The threat will always be there," Maggie whispered.

I swore. "Running means we're never going to be safe," I realized, slumping back into the couch. At least, we'd never be able to relax, to let down our guard. And Eva and Maggie deserved better than that.

Maggie urged me to scoot closer to Eva so she could sit down on my other side, meaning I was wedged tight between them on the small sofa. "So, how're we doing this?" Maggie asked, all business.

"What do you mean?" I asked, frowning at her. "You two aren't doing anything; you're staying out of this and staying safe."

Eva and Maggie started laughing in tandem. "I'm serious!" I exclaimed, trying to look sternly at both of them. "This is going to be very dangerous, and I don't want you mixed up with any of it."

Eva leaned in and kissed my cheek. "You're so funny Seph, thinking you have a say in this."

"*I'm serious!*" I shouted again, getting angry. I took a deep breath to calm myself and tried again. "I appreciate that you want to help. Really, I do. But I can't risk you. If either of you got hurt that..." I swallowed around the lump in my throat. "That would kill me."

Eva smiled at me sadly. "That's exactly why we want to help though, hun. If something happens to you that's going to hit us just as hard. We'll go crazy with worry if we can't help. There has to be *something* we can do that's low-risk but still helpful to you. We can—we can talk to the Collective people, vouch for your character and conduct. We can get married and make you an Earth citizen so they can't take you away." Her gray eyes turned pleading, and my heart broke at the idea that in order to keep her safe I probably wouldn't be able to keep her. Hadn't the universe taken enough from me? Hadn't I had enough shit to deal with? Why did I have to give up my salvation as soon as I'd found it?

But one thing in particular that she'd said snagged in my

mind. "You would...you would marry me? After everything I've told you? Even knowing what I am?"

Eva blushed, shrugging. "Yeah, I would. Especially if it keeps you safe. I know we haven't known each other long but it feels like I've known you for ages, somehow. Does that make sense? Probably not, as soon as I said it out loud it seemed kind of crazy—"

"No, it makes perfect sense. I feel the same way." My brow lowered as I considered if what she was describing was something like the mate bond. Could humans even experience it? It wasn't a universal phenomenon; most species didn't have anything like it. I licked my lips, considering. "Actually, there's something that can happen sometimes. It's not common, but both of my lineages have it and I think...I think it's happened to me. But I'm not sure, yet."

A crease formed between her brows. "What is it?"

I swallowed. "It's called...um, the mate bond. It's pretty rare but I think there are several Earth animals that mate for life, and this is a bit like that. Both yvrenii and felicans feel it. And that's what my parents were—my pa was yvrenii and my mom was felican. But there's a blood test I can do to determine if it's true. It checks for elevated levels of certain hormones."

She blinked at me, absorbing that, while Maggie whistled low on my other side. "Wow, you guys are like, cute little penguins or something. Not swans though; swans are too angry."

"Maybe I'm a swan, then, and your mom is a penguin." I was having trouble remembering which animals those were, but I was pretty sure they were birds.

Maggie considered, tapping her chin. "No, wait! You're a

goose, Seph, and Mom's one of those little parrots. Lovebirds?" She went back to her phone, searching for pictures of the animals she was describing. She showed me a picture of a large-looking bird with a long white neck and orange beak opened wide in a silent scream, teeth serrating the edge. "See, that's you." I laughed. "And this is Mom." Next she showed me a much softer and sweeter looking bird, snuggled up cozily beside another that looked just like it.

"You're really good at this," I told her, realizing that the brightly colored little birds did somehow remind me of Eva. "That's you two just living your lives and being adorable and then here I come screaming and bringing trouble."

"But also making things interesting," Maggie said, elbowing me gently.

"You two are something else," Eva smiled. "Hey, if this mate bond is so rare, does the Collective protect it at all?" she asked, her thick brows adorably wrinkled.

"Uh...yeah, I think so. I know true mates can't be separated. Why, what are you thinking, gorgeous?"

"Well, if we really are mates, and they're protected, we can probably use that when we talk to these guys, right? Make sure you stay with us. How do they test for it?"

I searched my memory. "I think it's just the blood test. There's a machine at my place that can run the ones that check for the mate bond hormones." I got to my feet, holding my hands out to the two females who had thoroughly stolen my heart and soul. "We can all go now. And—and find out."

Eva's stormcloud eyes searched my face, still feeling too bare without the helix skin draped over it. My heart beat a wild tempo in my chest, too nervous to even breathe as I waited for what she'd say. When she smiled and took my hand, letting me help her up, the relief was so intense I felt faint.

"Yeah. Let's do this," she said, keeping hold of my hand and squeezing it tight. "Let's go find out if we're mates."

Chapter 12

How the Other Half Lives

<u>EVA</u>

Seph got a strange look on his face, and the flickering hexagon pattern from before flowed over his skin, transforming him from someone Other to the Seth we'd come to know and love. A part of me that I didn't want to focus on too deeply was almost disappointed in seeing him look totally human again. There'd been something...wild about his true form that had captured my attention and wouldn't let it go.

"Oh snap, you know what? The grandma car makes a lot more sense now," Maggie said as we clambered into the pale gold sedan.

"And why is that?" Seph asked, shooting her a glance in the rearview mirror.

"Because you're an alien. You don't know that guys that look like you are supposed to drive motorcycles and muscle cars. Or at *least* an obnoxiously huge pickup truck."

He snorted. "Awful rude of you to profile me. I can like leather jackets *and* cozy little cars that get me where I'm going without drawing too much attention. *Ma'am*."

Maggie giggled. "Touché."

It was only about fifteen minutes before we were pulling up to a cute yellow brick bungalow on a quiet street. Kids were playing some game on the front lawn of a house two doors down that involved a lot of screaming and tumbling. I smiled, remembering when Maggie was that small and trying to turn every moment into a death-defying display of agility.

He led us up the front steps and unlocked the door. Then we were in, stepping over the threshold of my alien boyfriend's home.

I found myself confused by what I encountered, because it didn't look any different from how a normal house would look. It even had the same hallmarks of bachelorhood: mismatched furniture, colors too dark, too many things on the floor, and very little guest seating. If I hadn't already seen his true form I might have wondered if he was pulling my leg.

"This doesn't look alien at all," Maggie huffed, plopping down onto the only seating in the living room, a ratty-looking fold-out futon. "Where's the holograms and the glowing tubes?"

"Can't leave them out where just anyone could see 'em," Seph chuckled, going up to a touchpad on the wall and typing something in. The glass in the windows darkened, though I could still see out of them to the street beyond, and after another couple of seconds a faint humming pressed against my eardrums before fading away.

When I looked back at Seph he was no longer wearing his human skin (a truly ghoulish sentence to be thinking) and he was walking toward the fake fireplace on one wall. He reached into the recess, fumbling for something on the top. I heard a metallic pop, and then the front of the mantle was swinging outward—a secret compartment, apparently.

Once the hatch had swung open a few small lights flickered on inside, revealing a stash of weapons and tech straight out of a sci-fi movie.

I knew my mouth was hanging open, but I couldn't seem to properly close it. Knowing he was an alien mercenary and seeing the proof of it were two *very* different things. I couldn't believe one guy needed this many different ways to kill a person: there were knives and guns ranging in size from "small enough for a child" to "could double as a bludgeon", coils of wicked razor wire and cording, a crossbow and at least two quivers of arrows, and several instruments that looked like they were just tubes that I had nothing from Earth to compare them to.

"Holy *shit*, dude," Maggie breathed, reaching out for a particularly sharp-looking curved blade. I grabbed her wrist and tugged her back from the armory hiding in Seph's fake fireplace.

"No touchy," I told her firmly.

"Yeah, best not," Seph added sheepishly, reaching into the waistband of his pants and pulling a sheathed knife out that he added to the pile, before crouching down to lift his pant leg and remove a holster with a small pistol. Most unsettlingly, he then removed a necklace with a simple silver pendant on it that I'd seen him wear multiple times by now and add that, too. Then he closed the secret compartment and held his hands out from his sides. "So uh...want me to show you around first, or...?"

I smiled weakly, mentally shaking myself from my stunned silence. "Yeah, that sounds good."

Seph led us on a quick tour of his house, which was very bare and empty but overall roomy and pleasant. There were a lot of windows, and warm honey-brown hardwood throughout. The kitchen was surprisingly modern, with stainless steel appliances and nice granite countertops.

The house was much too big for him, most of the rooms empty or just a handful of things scattered around. There were three bedrooms and two baths, but he only used one of each, the ones in the main suite. "Why'd you get something so big?" I asked as he led us into the basement, where he'd said his medbay was stored. "Were you expecting more people to join you?"

He shrugged, the tips of his pointed ears darkening in a blush. "I guess I didn't realize just how big it was going to be. I bought it sight unseen, more or less."

The basement was a little less barren than the rest of the house, and there was a lot more stuff down here that didn't look quite right: crates and containers made of sleek metals and plastics like something out of a cyberpunk setting, a device that looked like a satellite array but with a strange shape to it instead of the curved dish, and in one corner, a coffin-like chamber that had to be the medbay.

Seph led us over to the shiny black shell that looked a little like a tanning bed, but with a glass window on top. He tapped the lid and a holographic display beamed into existence in front of his face. I couldn't read the language it was written in, but Seph flicked through its menus quickly, making selections. He hit one last button (if you could even still call something that insubstantial a button) and the lid cracked open with a hiss. A soothing melody played as the inside of the medbay revealed itself. The interior was a sterile white, little lights allowing a view of all the tubes and minuscule robotic arms that covered the inside of the lid. One particularly thick tube slid out of the snarl and extended towards Seph, who met the tube with the tip of his finger, slipping it into the opening. Something whirred, then snicked, and Seph jumped slightly. Then the tube retracted, and another holographic display showed an animated alien character thinking in an exaggerated manner. After a few seconds, the cartoon changed to a smiley face, and a readout of the results started scrolling across the screen.

Seph read it quietly, then turned to me and waved me closer. He took my hand, lacing our fingers together. "You see this?" he asked, pointing to a value. I couldn't read the words, but the numbers were the same as ours, and there were four values that were red.

I nodded. "What's it mean?"

Seph let out his breath slowly, squeezing my hand. "These four values, those are my oxytocin, dopamine, serotonin, and unamarin levels. All elevated."

My brow scrunched in confusion. "I recognize the first three, but what's that last one? And what does it mean?"

He swallowed audibly. "Well, unamarin is a hormone, like the other three. Yvrenii and felicans both produce it, but not very many other species. It's...the mate hormone. When we find our other halves a gland in our brain starts producing it and flooding our systems, which also causes the other three hormones to spike."

"So we are," I breathed, reaching out to cup his face. "You're my mate. This proves it, right?"

He shrugged, making my heart plummet. "It proves that you are *my* mate, but the Collective might not grant us protection because you probably won't have it, and the laws surrounding one-sided matings are a little less robust. With me being a criminal..."

"Test me," I demanded, thrusting my finger into his face. "Maybe humans can produce it too and we just haven't discovered it yet. Because I've never felt like this before, Seph. Never in my whole goddamn life. So—so try."

He pressed his plush lips into a hard line, causing his tusks to press painfully against the inside of his bottom lip. Then he gave me a curt nod and turned back to the holographic screen, dismissing the readout and navigating the menus again. Only this time he went somewhere else and after a few seconds the readout changed to English. I blinked, surprised, then smiled shakily.

"I can read it now," I said, amazed.

"Yeah, uh...I uploaded the English from my translator. Thought uh...thought you should be able to read it yourself."

I leaned in and kissed his cheek, touched. "Thank you. That was very thoughtful."

He grumbled something I didn't catch as he navigated over to the diagnostic tests and selected "hormone panel" from a list. Just like before, the thick tube emerged and stretched towards us, and once it had paused I reached out my hand and slotted my finger into the end just like Seph had. After a moment I felt a sharp pinch that made me suck in a shocked breath, and then something cool coated the end of my finger and the tube withdrew. The cute little cartoon alien came back and thought for a while, and then the results blazed across the screen.

I ignored most of it, looking for any red numbers. My heart started pounding in my chest when I realized there were four, just like for Seph's results: oxytocin, dopamine, serotonin, and unamarin.

He gasped, whipping around to face me. His three golden eyes searched my face intently, looking for something I hoped he'd see. Tears gathered in my eyes, and a huge smile stretched across my face. I let out a sobbing bark of laughter, then launched myself at him like a woman possessed.

But he caught me, his powerful arms catching my thighs before sliding to my ass to hold me in place against him. I wrapped my arms tight around his neck and proceeded to kiss the hell out of him.

Maggie was unusually generous for a fourteen-year-old, letting us have a moment for several seconds before she started making gagging noises. But I'd underestimated Sephyr, who saw her gags and raised her more intense kissing noises, sounding like he was trying to eat me, or perhaps suck me up through a straw.

I broke the kiss to start laughing, deep belly laughs that I had to stifle with my hand so I didn't blow out Seph's ear drums. He set me down carefully, giving me another peck on the cheek before striding over to Maggie to wrap her in a big bear hug. My daughter went stiff, her eyes widening over his shoulder, but after a moment I saw her give a wobbly smile and hug him back.

"Alright, well. That's settled, then," Seph said roughly. His two main eyes looked more than a little glassy, making my heart melt in my chest.

"So that means you can't just up and leave us," I told him, lifting my chin and trying to look intimidating. "It's—it's illegal. You have to let us help you."

He frowned at me. "I'm not putting you in danger, Eva. That's non-negotiable for me."

I sighed. "Then we won't *be* in danger. We'll be careful." I urged my child closer, putting my hand on her shoulder when she was finally standing beside me. "I think Maggie's idea was a really good one. We go to your government and see if they can't do something. We have proof now that we're mates, and that's something we can try to use to protect ourselves and stay together, right? I really think it could work."

Seph's mouth twisted as he considered. "It might. It might also blow up in our faces and they'll arrest you alongside me just to keep the peace. You're not supposed to know about us, remember? If they throw us all in a cell that's still keeping us together, technically."

Doubt crept in. "They'd do that?"

He snorted. "Of course they would; they're a government, not a charity."

I felt myself sag, the bright hope I'd been clinging to dimming. I felt like an idiot.

"*Vrakaash*, I didn't mean it like that, Eva." He stepped closer, grabbing my biceps and squeezing them comfortingly. "My experiences with the law might be coloring my responses, here. It *is* a good idea, sweetheart. I just don't know if they'll let me go, even with a mate and child vouching for me and trying to protect me."

"Well, the only other idea we've had is just as risky. Running and hiding and hoping that it's enough isn't exactly rock solid," I snapped.

He sighed, ruffling his hair. "Alright, you've got me there. Maybe we should table this for a little while, huh? Let me make you some dinner."

"I could eat," Maggie chipped in.

"Alright, sure. Let's get some food in us and see if we can't come up with anything better."

Chapter 13

Sleepover Party!

<u>EVA</u>

True to his word, Sephyr ushered us upstairs and insisted we watch TV while he threw together a meal for us. Which, yes, did absolutely win him some points, but I was suspicious of how abruptly he'd cut off our discussion. It was getting a little late, but not so late that he needed to insist on dinner right then.

"He's up to something," Maggie murmured, cranking up the volume on the TV to cover our talking.

"Okay, but I was *just* thinking that same thing." The apple had not fallen far from the tree *at all*. "Hopefully whatever it is we can talk him out of it."

Maggie nodded, looking grim. "Yeah. He's kind of...dumb. Emotionally."

I sighed, nodding. "Yup. Figures that the first decent guy I meet winds up being an alien with a masochistic streak." I licked my lips, darting a look at the kitchen, where sizzling and faint rock music I didn't recognize were trickling out to us under the sound of the TV. "How do you feel about all this stuff, kiddo? I mean...it's a lot, and you were already having a tough day."

She nodded, considering. "I don't know, but I think overall...happy. I really like Seth—Seph—and I think he's good for you, even if he *is* an idiot. I think..." she swallowed, looking away. The next thing she said was so quiet I wasn't even sure if I was hearing her right. "I don't think I'd mind if he was my...my dad."

Tears threatened. "Really?" I couldn't help but ask around the lump in my throat. Maggie was so hesitant around people, and the fact that she'd liked him from the get-go spoke volumes about what kind of guy Seph was. More than my own judgment, I trusted my kid's.

She nodded, smiling faintly. "Yeah. The vibes are immaculate."

I nodded. "Yeah, we'll have to teach him what it means to be a part of a family. Show him how it's done." I held out my hand out towards Maggie, palm up, and she dutifully slapped it.

Seph poked his head out of the kitchen, his mop of curly copper hair pushed back from his face by a thin black headband, making his third eye and pointed ears more prominent. "You guys want salad with the chicken and green beans? I got this mix at the store that has fruit in it, too."

"That does actually sounds really good. Mags?"

She wrinkled her nose. "Fruit in salads is sacrilege."

I chuckled, turning back to Seph, who was also grinning. "I'm down, so we can just split it."

He nodded, throwing me a wink. "You got it, gorgeous."

I should have been more unnerved by the fact that the man I'd been seeing was an alien. I should have found his three eyes and his russet fur and sharp teeth unnerving instead of adorable, should have found it repugnant instead of...sexy. But at the end of the day, it was just stuff that made Seph who he was, parts of him that weren't ugly, just different, and it didn't stop me from loving him.

Didn't stop me from being his mate.

Phew, what a fucking bombshell, I thought, cleaning my nails absently. Thirty-five years with no one I could see myself saying forever to only to stumble head-first into someone who not only *felt* like my perfect match, but seemed to be literally, biologically perfect for me. Somehow. I'd have to read up on the mate bond. Maybe there was an alien internet that Seph could let me use. I had a ton of shit I wanted (and needed) to read up on: the Collective, the two species that Seph was, maybe even...how we could move to an alien planet. Aside from Maggie and the comfort of the familiar, there wasn't much for me here, and I suspected that Seph wouldn't be allowed to stay here once we reached out to his government. Would Maggie be okay with it? She liked her routines, but I knew my poor baby was struggling, too. Coming out had made it so hard for her to find a place to fit in in the real world —she found like-minded people on the internet, but at school, it was a different story. Maybe alien planets would be more welcoming of her. More understanding.

"Alright, ladies—dinner is served!" Seph called from the kitchen. I turned off the TV and shook off my thoughts; it was too early for that, anyway.

Dinner was lovely, but more lovely still was how we all got to just...relax and chill afterward, enjoying each other's company. I helped Seph clean up, tackling the dishes while he wiped up the stove and counters. It had been a simple meal but *my god* had he made a mess. He finished before me, coming up behind me and pressing his front to my back and wrapping his arms tight around my middle.

"You want me to help over here at all, *pra'ja*?" he rumbled in my ear, making goosebumps pebble my arms and causing something low in my belly to heat.

"No, I'm almost done. But thank you." I turned my head to kiss his cheek. "What does that mean, by the way? *Pra'ja*? I think you've called me that before."

He grunted a laugh, resting his chin on my shoulder. "It's a felican word. I heard my mom say it to my dad a lot. It's a...special term. For uh, mates. I'm not sure what it means exactly. Should probably look it up, huh?"

"It's pretty, I like it," I told him. Something about what he'd said jogged my memory then. "Oh! By the way, I was wondering if there was a way for me to look up information on whatever you aliens use instead of the internet. I want to read up on *so* much stuff. Everything I can, really."

"Sure. I'll grab my tablet and configure it for English. The nexus access is really limited this far out, but you can still get on the Encyclopedia and certain government-run sites."

"Perfect!" I slotted the last newly-cleaned plate into the dish rack and spun in his arms, cupping his face for a kiss. "You don't mind my using your stuff?"

He shook his head. "Nah. Can't keep secrets from my mate," he murmured against my lips. I melted into him, the heat from his strong body seeping into me like sunshine. I studied his face, searching for anything that might spell trouble: uncertainty, nerves, resentment. But I came up empty.

"You really mean that, don't you?" I asked, breathless.

He nuzzled his nose into mine, dropping a sweet kiss onto my lips. "I do. The mate bond is sacred, Eva. It's rare. I'm not all that smart but I'd have to be a special kind of dumb to screw *that* up."

I smiled, swallowing around a lump in my throat. He pressed one last lingering kiss to my lips, his taste flooding my senses and making my mouth water, before pulling away to lead me into the living room to join Maggie. Seph slipped away to grab his tablet, switching the display to English just like he had the medbay downstairs.

I spent entirely too long geeking out about it, because while it was rather like an Earth tablet..it was also very different. It was largely holographic, and when it was off it looked like a picture frame with the glass knocked out of it, a black rectangule that looked like plastic but had the heft of metal. And then once it was on you'd swear you were holding a regular tablet, the screen was so crisp and rich with detail, and hardly translucent at all. But there was no glass, no screen, everything projected and incorporeal, like all of the other alien tech I'd seen from Seph.

"I want one," I breathed, having the time of my life just flicking through menus.

He laughed, showing me which icon opened the internet browser—or, rather, the "nexus port".

"Anything for you, gorgeous," he chuckled. I sank into his side, snuggling up against him while I started running searches for what I wanted to know. Seph split his attention between what I was up to, telling me how to spell things and answering my questions, and the trashy reality TV show that Maggie was watching. I didn't really like those shows—my amusement came more from how Maggie reacted to the ridiculous things happening on screen—but Seph seemed genuinely interested, trading guesses and gossip with my daughter like he'd been watching it for years.

He fit into our little family so well. It was amazing that something genetic could get something like that so right.

Time got away from us, and before we knew it it was midnight, and me and Maggie were both falling asleep on the couch.

"You wanna just spend the night?" Seph asked as he gently prodded me awake. "You and Maggie can take my bed and I'll camp out in one of the spare rooms."

I waved him away with a yawn. "We can't put you out of your bed," I protested. I looked over at Maggie, who hadn't even twitched from our conversation. "Why don't we let her sleep here on the couch and you and me can take the bed?"

Heat flared in his three golden eyes. "You think she'll be comfortable out here?"

"Oh, yeah. It's a nice couch, and Maggie likes couches. Sometimes when I get up in the morning she's out in the living room instead of her room." I bit my lip, his eyes tracking the movement hungrily. "I want to spend the night with you," I whispered, swaying ever so slightly closer to him.

His throat bobbed, golden eyes burning into me like sweet fire. Finally he nodded, pulling a blanket out of an ottoman to drape over Maggie, then taking me by the hand. He led me through the still, dark house to his bedroom, which was fairly bare, just like the rest of the house. But it did have a little bit more softness to it, and was steeped in his scent.

Heart pounding, I slid the door shut after us and pushed in the lock on the knob. Seph's hand had gone clammy in mine, his shoulders stiff, and I realized that he was nervous. Surely he wasn't a virgin? He was so...so *cocky* up until now. It didn't seem possible. "Are you okay?" I asked softly, stepping closer and taking his other hand.

He let out a shaky breath, his throat flushing with nerves. "You got me all choked up, gorgeous. Like I've never been with a female before in my life." His two main eyes slid down to stare at the floor, his third eye peeking at me from the corner. "I just...I guess I don't want to mess it up. Like I have everything else."

My chest shattered at how scared and vulnerable he sounded. Seph was a guy who'd been hurt in life—*a lot*. And he'd gotten so used to it that he was expecting it now. He might have even believed he deserved it.

I cupped his face, running my thumbs along his high cheekbones and smiling at him, even though he still wasn't quite looking at me. "And how exactly are you planning on ruining things?" I asked.

Finally, he looked at me. "You never plan to ruin things, gorgeous. They just kind of...fall apart."

I nodded, still holding him. "Sure. But we got something special, you and me. Only one in ten thousand couples have the mate bond, according to what I was reading earlier." I slid my hands down, caressing his neck, his shoulders, before pressing my palms into his broad chest, the staccato beating of his heart thrumming into my skin. "I'm here. I'm yours. And I want you. You might be the first person I've ever wanted in my entire life like this. So please...love me."

He looked at me like my words had hurt him, like I'd taken a knife and started flaying him alive. But when I tilted my chin towards him, silently begging for his kiss, he gave it to me, his mouth crashing into mine. He clutched at me tightly, moaning low in his throat like my lips were the best thing he'd ever tasted. His fingers carded into my hair, fisting it gently at the back of my head and locking me in place right where he wanted me.

I cupped his face again, wanting him to feel how I cherished him, how much I cared for him, loved him, exactly as he was, fuzzy three-eyed orc and everything.

I pressed closer, fitting my body tight against his and gasping into his mouth when I felt the hard bar of his shaft pressing into my hip. I threw my arms around his neck for balance, then hitched a leg up so that I could grind my aching core against him, the embers of arousal flaring hot and bright as soon as I'd felt the proof of his desire.

He groaned, big warm hands grabbing at my generous ass and pressing me harder against him as his mouth slanted and his textured tongue swept into my mouth, licking into me with desperation as we ground our sexes together.

Between one breath and the next I was spinning, flying through the air in a confusing jumble, landing on the mattress with a surprised huff of air. Before I could orient myself and parse through what had happened Seph was on me, his knee wedging itself between my thighs, pressing against my needy clit with delicious friction. His mouth slanted over mine once more, claiming my mouth, claiming *me*, with bold strokes of his tongue and stinging nips that he quickly soothed away. He was winding me so tight, bringing me close to the edge already with both of us still fully clothed.

One of his hands found my breast, kneading it and making me cry out into his mouth at just how good his hand felt there. He broke the kiss with a dark chuckle that made me clench on nothing. "Careful, gorgeous," he admonished, his sinfully full lips tugging into a grin that flashed his fangs. "Don't want Maggie to hear, do you?"

He dipped his head, nuzzling along my jawline until he hit the sensitive spot behind my ear that drove me wild. Then he stayed there, driving my pleasure to unthinkable heights with tongue and lips and teeth until I was certain I'd soaked straight through my panties into my jeans. I writhed and panted under him, one hand fisted into his curly ginger hair while the other started trying to pull his shirt up. I needed his skin on mine, needed to see him, all of him, and show him all of me. All of the parts that I had been so sure were ugly that he'd kissed and told me were beautiful.

He pulled away from my neck, sitting up and resting on his heels so he could peel his dark gray shirt off, and when I saw him in all his glory I stopped breathing.

Seth had been hot, but Sephyr was a thing of beauty. He was the perfect blend of soft and hard that had my mouth watering, his well-bronzed skin stretched over muscle softened with fat in a way that just made him look juicy, good enough to sink my teeth into. His fur was fairly sparse on his chest and belly, but the coppery color of it was bright against his darker skin, limning him in the low light of his bedroom. Scars of his own twisted like pale ribbons over his skin, marks left by the difficult things he'd had to do to make it this far. I sucked in a breath, reaching out to gently stroke the faint collar of scar tissue around his throat.

"What happened here, Seph?" I asked softly.

His hand came up to join my fingers in exploring the old wound. "Bounty went bad. Guy tried to garrote me because he thought I was full-felican, but yvrenii have these thick cartilage plates under the skin that protect the throat, so all he managed was scratching me up pretty bad." He swallowed, his three golden eyes dimming and going somewhere far away for a moment. But he shook it off, looking at me again and raising one eyebrow at my clothes, as if to ask *well? What are you waiting for?* It made his third eye scrunch on one side, a fact which I immediately decided was adorable as hell.

I reached down and tugged my own shirt off, arching my back to be able to rip it over my head. Back still arched, I also reached back to undo my bra, just managing it with an embarrassing pop of my shoulder. All three of his eyes were rapt on what my hands were doing, his own still and seemingly glued to the waistband of his jeans. When I peeled my bra off and flung it away he shuddered, which seemed to break him out of whatever he was trapped in.

He dove into my chest, his hot mouth latching onto one dark nipple while his hand cupped my other breast. I sucked in a breath, the dual stimulation driving me wild, making my hips buck desperately into him. He lavished the sensitive tips with attention, sucking and licking one while toying with the other with his fingers, alternating periodically, until I was a panting mess, softly begging him for more: "Please, Seph," I gasped.

"Please what, *pra'ja*?" he purred, grinning down at me.

"I-I need you," I whined, rolling my pelvis up into his.

"Mmm," he hummed, his hand sliding down my body to rub my throbbing clit through my pants, making me gasp and whimper. I didn't think I'd ever whimpered before in my whole life. "Does this pretty pussy need me to take care of it? You want me to taste you, gorgeous? Because I think if I don't get you on my tongue soon I'm going to lose my mind."

Oh sweet Jesus, I thought, my brain short-circuiting and stopping me from saying anything. All I managed was a nod, my hands trying to squeeze between our bodies so I could rip my pants off, but Seph grabbed my wrists, stopping me. He tsked, shaking his head and grinning wolfishly. "You better not," he growled, forcing my hands up to the headboard and coaxing me to grab the wooden slats. "You move your hands from here and we're going to have to have words. You hear me?" I nodded, breathless and helpless but to obey. "Good girl," he purred, and fuck me but I never would have guessed I was so *into* that.

His hands slid down my body, leaving tingling goosebumps in their wake, before he undid the button of my jeans and slid my panties down with the denim, baring me to his hungry gaze.

I had a moment of insecurity then though, the fire in my blood dimming. With my arms up and my legs splayed every scar was on display, every imperfectly groomed patch of body hair that I couldn't shave without risking a painful flareup, out in the open. I did my best to ignore the feelings, but Seph must have sensed something was wrong, because despite his threats he didn't say anything when I lowered my arms except to ask me what was wrong.

I shrugged a shoulder, squeezing my knees together and keeping my elbows tucked against my sides. "It's nothing, I'm just...being silly."

He frowned, laying down beside me. He combed back my long dark hair, playing with the strands before kissing me softly. "Don't give me that, gorgeous. What's going on in that pretty head of yours?"

I bit my lip. "Well that's it, isn't it?" I blurted, my eyes slipping from his in shame. "I'm not gorgeous. Not really. I've got all these scars and wounds and hair..."

"Ah," he replied, kissing me again. "I see, so you've lost

your mind, then. Don't worry, I'll help you find it." Then he took my wrists again and forced them up, his molten gold eyes raking over me, taking in the red twisted scars, the active sites in my right armpit that were scabbing over but still tender. Then he shook his head, rolling onto his back so he could undo his pants and kick them off, revealing his hard, flushed length to my greedy eyes. He gestured at his cock, which twitched and drooled precum under my appreciative gaze. "This look like it bothers me in the slightest?"

When I remained silent he rolled back onto his side, cupping my face and kissing me again, his lips so soft yet firm on mine. "Stay in the moment with me, Eva," he murmured against my lips, his hand sliding from my face to cup my breast again. "Whoever told you there was something wrong with how you look because of your condition isn't here. *I am.* And I think you look good enough to eat. Let me love you," he rasped, echoing my earlier words and making me melt.

I swallowed around the lump in my throat and nodded, throwing my arms around his neck and clutching him in a desperate hug. "I love you, Sephyr," I whispered into his throat. He groaned, pulling me close and clutching at me hard enough I felt the prick of claws.

"I...I love you too, Eva. So damn much. Are you okay?"

I nodded, pulling back to meet his eyes. It was still a little disorienting trying to look into three at once but I was getting used to it. "Yes. I...I want to see you. All of you. Can I—can I touch you?"

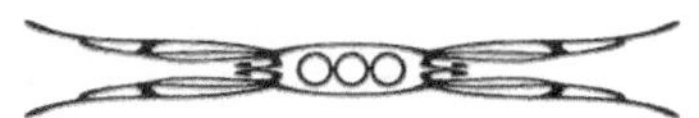

SEPHYR

Can I touch you? As if every atom of my being wasn't screaming at me to touch her, taste her, sink my cock so deep into her my sleeve would swallow up her clit and suckle it.

"'Course you can, baby," I said roughly, laying on my back again. I knew it made me a hypocrite, but I couldn't help the wave of insecurity that stole over me as she swept her stormcloud gaze over my body. I wasn't exactly yvrenii or felican, and I certainly wasn't human, but she'd said she loved me, and I had to trust that my mate, of all people, would see my many flaws and call them beautiful. She'd been so brave for me, and I owed it to her to at least try and stop myself from expecting her to turn to me in disgust.

Her fingers trailed over my chest, her slim fingers combing through the sparse patches of fur and making shivers course up and down my spine. She caressed my pectorals, circling my pierced nipple with a smirk that made me want to bite something. Her fingers trailed lower, reverently tracing the lines of my well-padded muscles. She traced the silvery twists of my scars, clucking in sympathy and pressing soft kisses to the biggest ones.

Her eyes slid lower before her hands did, eyeing my achingly hard cock with hungry eyes. The swollen, heavily leaking thing jumped under her gaze, eager for her attention. But her eyes snagged on my weeping sleeve first, one finger descending to rim the wet pucker. When it twitched and gaped for her finger she gasped, but didn't pull away.

"What's this?" she asked, curiosity and something hotter spiking her voice.

"It's called a sleeve. Yvrenii females have a prod instead of a clit. It's kind of like a mix between a clit and a dick. So when two yvrenii mate there's...mutual penetration."

"Hoo boy, that's..." I braced, praying she wasn't about to reject me. "That's so *hot*." She leaned down, replacing her finger with that devilish little tongue of hers. She gave me a slow, swirling lick, making the breath leave my lungs. Only for it to come rushing back in when she slipped her tongue past the ring of muscle, inside of me, and I was not prepared for it. All of the non-yvrenii females I'd been with hadn't been interested in doing this; if my sleeve had gotten any attention it was with fingers.

"Eva..." I ground out, unable to stop my hips from twitching up towards her mouth, something in me snapping and going desperate. She loosed a husky chuckle, sinking her tongue further and groaning, sending a jolt of sensation through me that shot up my spine and set my brain alight with pleasure.

And then her hand wrapped around my cock, and I was lost.

I knew that I was shaped differently from human males, my member more curved and with a narrower tip that ballooned into a thicker base—not quite a knot, because it didn't inflate outside of my base arousal, but somewhat close in shape. And I was heavily textured all over with little bumps that human males also seemed to lack.

Eva's hand glided smoothly over my hot flesh, thanks to the natural lube I produced, and the squeeze and flex of her fingers on my shaft was unreal. She'd found exactly the balance between rough and gentle that drove me wild, and I felt my nuts wrench up against the base of my shaft, my orgasm threatening already, when she combined a squeeze of the sensitive head with a swirling lick of my sleeve.

I sat up, easing her off of me and flipping us so that she

was on her back underneath me once more. "Not so fast, gorgeous," I growled, sliding down her body. "Can't have you making this end too early. I've got to savor this." I grinned down at her, so flushed and dazed. "Put those hands back where I want them."

She obeyed wordlessly, and I slapped the side of her hip lightly, grinning as I forced my body between her spread thighs, urging them wider. "Good girl," I grinned.

I slung one of her trembling legs over my shoulder, opening her up so that I could love every inch of her. She thought I found her scars disgusting? I'd show her just how wrong she was. I used one hand to trace her seam, gathering the copious slick there and rolling it over my fingers, saturating my skin with it. I eased a finger into her tight heat, groaning at how her inner walls clamped onto me. I used my thumb to rub circles on her swollen pearl of flesh, making her choke on a cry as she struggled to stay quiet. I lowered my head and started kissing at the bumpy red skin of her inner thigh, nuzzling the crease where her leg met her hip and where the scars were thickest, many of them twisted and still painful-looking.

"You think I could possibly look at all of this and think you're anything other than gorgeous?" I kissed around a healing wound carefully, my heart breaking for her pain but my cock still aching to sink into her. "You're crazy, babygirl." I removed my hand from her, making her mewl in protest, only to sink two fingers into her and latch onto her clit like she was my last meal.

She sucked in a breath, arching her back, and one of her hands went to my hair, finding my vestigial felican ears and stroking them. I shuddered, my stub of a tail going wild at the base of my spine, but I removed my mouth from her and nipped at the inside of her thigh, making her squeak. "What did I tell you about those hands?" I asked, my voice low and rough. "You want me to tie you up and spank you?"

"Yes," she breathed, squirming under me and biting her rosy lip. Had I thought my tail was going nuts before? Because it felt like it was going to fling itself right off my body, now.

I mentally shook myself, crooking my fingers inside of her. "Maybe next time, if you're good for me. I don't think I can wait long enough to tie you up." Then my mouth was too busy for talk, my tongue laving her clit, sucking on it. She panted and writhed under me, no longer coherent as I coaxed her to orgasm.

I felt her fluttering around my fingers, a soft whine trickling from her lips, and I increased my pressure, sending her tumbling over the edge with a cry she wasn't quite capable of silencing in time. I should have been concerned about Maggie hearing, but I'd detected no movement out in the living room since we'd left it, so hopefully after her long day the poor cub would sleep right through it all.

I kept working Eva, groaning at her scent, her flavor, feeling like her essence was rearranging my molecules so that she'd become an essential element for my survival. It felt like I'd never be able to get enough of her, like I might actually die without her. Soon she was clenching tight around me all over again, her face buried under a pillow to stifle her scream.

Technically she'd let go of the headboard to grab it, but I decided to allow it.

She gently pushed me away, her pale skin flushed and her steel gray eyes wild and glassy. Her legs were trembling and weak on either side of me, and I kissed her shivering thigh. "Damn, I thought you were gorgeous before," I told her, my voice thick with gravel, "but when you come for me you are absolutely *stunning*."

"Fucking hell, you and that mouth," she panted, struggling onto her elbows to look at me better. "Come here. I need you."

I stilled, my heart flying into my throat. *I need you.* Had anyone ever, in my entire life, needed me? "Anything for you, babygirl," I breathed, placing one more kiss on her thigh before sliding up her body until the head of my cock was lined up at her entrance. "You're sure you still want this?"

She smiled and nodded, cupping my face in that way she had that was so sweet it ached. Love shone from her eyes, and she pulled me down for a tender kiss. "Yes. I'm absolutely certain. I want you Seph—all of you. So don't keep me waiting anymore, yeah?"

I smiled down at her, nuzzling my nose into hers and pressing our foreheads together, the gentle pressure on my closed third eye feeling so right. "Yes, ma'am."

I reached down to take myself in hand, making sure I was lined up correctly, then pressed forward into her slick, silky heat with a groan that she echoed. Sensation barreled through me, stealing my breath and forcing me to hold still for a second. It had never been like this before, this intense, this...life-changing. Was this another facet of the mate bond? Would it be like this every time?—like I was having a religious experience, like I was coming home after being away for too long?

Frustrated with my stillness, Eva started moving under me, rolling her hips so that my length finished sliding inside her. "Fucking hell, gorgeous," I swore, shuddering at the feel of my shaft fully encased in her sweet cunt, her clit teasing my sleeve.

"You feel amazing," she gasped, her blunt nails digging into my back.

"So do you," I ground out, finally managing to gather enough of my wits about me to start moving again.

I'd heard males all my life talking about how they wanted a woman smaller than them, but I liked that me and Eva were the same size; everything lined up perfectly, and I could wrap her up tight in my arms even as I thrust in and out of her. I could kiss her as slow and deep as my strokes, could look her in the eyes and marvel at all the beauty of all the stars shining out at me from her face.

I pressed myself deep inside of her, burying my face in her neck and letting myself drown in her scent. "I love you. So fucking much," I rasped, clutching her close to me.

She held me back, just as tightly. "I love you, too," she murmured, her voice rough with tears. I pulled back to kiss her, her mouth opening for me and welcoming the slow glide of my tongue against hers. She raked her nails up and down my back, combing through the fur there, and for some reason that was what did me in: I snapped, some animal deep inside of me cutting itself loose and snarling with its need: the need to claim my mate, fill her full of my seed and brand her with my scent so no one would dare to try and take what was *mine.*

My Eva.

My mate.

My hips snapped forward, a feral growl rumbling deep in my chest. Eva's eyes widened, but the smile that curled her lips was pure sin. I rose up onto my knees, one hand latching onto her hip while the other cupped her leg under the knee and lifted it up off the bed. She cried out, tilting her head back so that her throat arched and strained, her dark eyes squeezing shut. Then I was pounding into her, setting a brutal pace that was making the bed creak and groan ominously. Eva was looking up at me with an expression that didn't know if it wanted to be desperate or stunned. Her eyes went unfocused, her channel tightening around my cock.

"That's it, gorgeous," I snarled, my hips snapping forward faster and faster, "I want you to come as hard as you can for me." She nodded, dazed, her hands still clenched tight around the slats of the headboard and her breasts rippling with the force of our motion. Her eyes rolled back, a low groan starting up in her chest, and I pressed the flat of my thumb between us, circling her clit, and then she was doing as I'd asked, clamping down on me so hard I could barely move, clenching me like a tight fist even as moisture pooled against my pelvis and dripped down the front of my legs. I ground my hips into her, removing my hand so my sleeve could latch onto her clit, and then I was following her over the edge, roaring her name even as she screamed mine into her pillow and came again, milking me for all I was worth.

I didn't think I'd ever come so hard in my life, spurt after spurt shooting out of me and my sac yanked up so tight it almost hurt. Every time it felt like I should be done Eva would wriggle against me, her channel fluttering and tightening as the pulsing of my sleeve brought on another orgasm for her, which would trigger another small one for me, creating a constant feedback loop that only ended when we got too sensitive and forced ourselves apart.

Even though we were both damp with sweat I couldn't resist pulling her close and curling myself around her. She rested her head on my arm, nuzzling her nose into my chest and draping an arm over my side. She squirmed a little closer, wedging one leg between mine and draping the other over my hip. Satisfied, she let out a soft sigh and went boneless in my arms. I smiled, pressing a kiss into her damp hair and breathing in the smell of her sweat and the perfume of sex on the air.

We lay in silence, trading little kisses and letting our heart rates settle.

<u>EVA</u>

I'd never had sex like *that* before in my whole life, and I was horrified to find myself overwhelmed after. It had been pleasurable, of course—I didn't know I could come so hard until Seph had started doing his damnedest to eat me alive—but more than that it was…present. Attentive. Emotional. And I was feeling a lot of things about it that I couldn't quite understand.

It was like that, sometimes: the harder I tried to grab onto my thoughts and feelings the more they slipped away, panicking under my scrutiny and dispersing like mist in the wind. All I could really tell was that I was Feeling A Lot, and I was bracing for him to notice and get frustrated with me. That was what usually happened.

I burrowed in tighter against him, wriggling closer and pressing my face into his shoulder in the blind hope that it would somehow help me get a grip on myself. Seph's fingers paused in the little trails they'd been tracing up and down my arms and back. "You alright, gorgeous?" he asked, pressing a kiss into the top of my head.

I tensed, keeping my face hidden. "Yeah, I'm fine." Because I was. It had been a positive experience and I'd enjoyed it, and I was fairly confident that on the other side of whatever this was, I'd be elated.

He grunted. "Don't *seem* fine. Did I do something to hurt you? You have to tell me now; it's illegal to lie to your mate."

That got me. I lifted my head, looking into his face. He was trying so hard to be cavalier about it, but I could tell he was also feeling very vulnerable right now. His eyes searched mine with a kind of frightened desperation, and that helped me snatch one of my feelings as it tried to flap past me yet again. "You did nothing wrong. *Nothing.*" I leaned down to kiss him, begging him with my lips on his to believe me, to understand. When I pulled away I settled on his shoulder again, my instinct still to hide from the big things I was feeling. "I guess…I'm just a little overwhelmed. In a good way! Like…it's never been that way for me before and I'm scared of what that means."

I felt him relax against me just a fraction, his arms tightening and pulling me closer. "How so?"

I thought about it, and I was unspeakably glad that he gave me that time to ponder and sort. "I think I'm mad that I'm thirty-five and this is the first time I'm having good sex. Because I deserved better." He slapped the outside of my thigh, draped across his own legs, soothing the skin carefully to work out the small sting.

"Damn straight, you did."

I thought again. "I think it's also kind of scary because…

because I don't want to lose it. It was so wonderful—*you're* so wonderful—but things are so uncertain right now. What if I lose you when I've only just found you?"

Seph groaned, yanking me higher against him so he could tilt my chin up for another kiss. "You are so goddamn precious, *pra'ja,*" he murmured against my lips, nuzzling my nose with his. "I get that. I really do. I'm not…I'm not used to things staying good for me. I can't think of another time in my life I've been as happy as I've been since I met you and Maggie. Maybe before my parents died, but that's it. Twenty-four, almost twenty-five years without having anything to keep going for but spite."

A sound somewhere between a whine and a moan ripped from my throat and I surged forward, wrapping him up tight in my arms. He stayed still for a moment—shocked, perhaps—before his arms snaked around me and held onto me tight, something shuddering through him as I rocked him as much as I could. It was more like I was jiggling him, but I didn't think he cared.

The silky heat of his skin against me, the thump of his heart beating in harmony with mine, became my whole world; it was everything: everything I'd ever wanted, ever needed, ever *would* need, and I let myself drown in it gladly. *This is the mate bond,* I thought in a daze. It had to be, because otherwise how could I explain how someone had become as essential to my survival as water and air in just a couple of weeks?

"I love you so much," he whispered in my ear, and I pressed kisses to every inch of him I could reach, too overwhelmed for words now, too lost in the tide of feeling ebbing and flowing between us. He pulled away from me, searching my face, and I gave him a smile, the brightest and most open one I could muster, willing everything I was feeling to shine through. He closed his eyes, giving me a wobbly smile back, then dipped his head to claim my lips in another kiss, this one heavier, achingly tender but desperate. He took careful sips and nibbles of my lips, letting me feel his tusks and fangs but not letting them hurt me.

I made a desperate sound in the back of my throat, my back arching to press me closer to him. One of his hands slid down to my leg, hefting it higher, and I felt the hard bar of his desire slide against my flesh.

I ripped my mouth from his, confusing him for a moment until I sat up and swung my leg all the way over to the other side of his hips so that I was straddling him, my still-throbbing pussy poised over his reawakened cock. Understanding dawned, and he grinned up at me, his eyes hooded but blazing with hunger. His hands went to my hips, guiding me down onto his hot and slippery length.

We gasped and groaned in tandem as he filled me, his three eyes locked on mine, flaying me open, stitching me back together, pulling me under. I rode him hard, maintaining that eye contact and relishing the feeling of drowning.

When we came it was together, eyes locked and sunk deep in each others' gaze.

Chapter 14

That Goddamn Dirty Rat

<u>EVA</u>

I'd fallen asleep in Sephyr's arms, but I woke up all alone in a big cold bed.

I lay still under the covers, which were tucked up tight under my chin, concealing my nudity. My ears strained for any sounds in the room besides my own, but even holding my breath I couldn't hear anything. There was some dull thumping from closer to the front of the house, though, so I threw off the covers and hurriedly got dressed. I slipped into the attached bathroom—this house really was *so* nice—and was touched to find a brand new toothbrush set out on the counter. It was baby blue, my favorite color.

Once I was as fresh as I could make myself I opened the door and made my way to the stairs. Maggie was up and watching TV, looking remarkably refreshed for her. It was rare that I was up after her—and if I was it was because she was still up from the night before, the poor baby.

"Is Seph in the kitchen?" I asked her, already heading back there.

But my daughter's next words stopped me and left me feeling cold. "No. He's not with you?" Those words hung in the air for a moment, squeezing the air from my lungs, and then I was racing for the kitchen, needing to see for myself that he wasn't there. When it proved as still and empty as Maggie had said I swore, turning for the basement door. Maybe he'd gone to do alien shit down there.

I threw the door open, my heart pounding in my ears almost as loudly as my feet on the old wood steps. "Seph?" I called out, heading to the corner with the medbay.

Silence was my only reply, but there was a lamp lit near the coffin-like machinery. Far off I heard Maggie calling for me, making her way down here to join me.

Once I was close I saw Seph's phone and tablet on a stool. There was a sticky note stuck to the phone screen: *Play the video.*

My stomach dropped, and my hand was shaking badly when I picked up the dark, lifeless rectangle. I just stood there, staring at it in my hand and begging the universe to let this not be what I thought it was.

Soon Maggie had joined me, calling my name with an edge of fear to her voice that snapped me out of the worst of my freeze. "Mom, what's going on? Where's Seph?" I turned to face her, so she could see the phone in my hand, and the note stuck to it.

Maggie swallowed around a sad little sound. "What's in the video?" she asked, glassy eyes meeting mine.

"I don't know yet, baby," I admitted in a whisper. "Do you want to watch it?"

She shook her head. "Hell no. But I think we gotta."

I nodded, removing the note and unlocking the phone with a swipe; he'd disabled his lock screen, apparently. It was already opened to the camera roll, and the very first icon was a still of Seph's face, looking grim, with the cellar wall behind him. I clicked on the icon, making sure the volume was up so we'd be able to hear the terrible news I could feel looming.

"Eva. Maggie. My two beautiful females," he began, making tears threaten at the backs of my eyes. "I don't know what to say except...I'm sorry. I'm sorry I'm such a *vrakaashaad*, so unworthy of you. But I love you anyway, both of you, and I know you'll hate me for this but...Veldar's tits, I couldn't put you at risk. I had to keep you as far away from the Collective and the brotherhood as possible, and that means doing the thing I promised I wouldn't do."

"That son of a bitch," Maggie hissed, and I grabbed her hand and clung to it, feeling the ground try and slip out from underneath me.

"By the time you see this I'll have rendezvoused with the Collective enforcer ship still in orbit to turn myself in and try and take down the brotherhood."

Maggie's hand clenched tighter around mine, and I pulled her in close against my side.

"I'm so, so sorry, my loves. I wish there would have been another way. Another way where I got to have it all, to have you safe and all three of us—" his voice broke, and it was several seconds before he was able to talk again, tears streaming from his two main eyes by the end of it. "For us to be a family," he finished in a sob. My heart was breaking, but it was like a shell cracking and breaking apart, something hot and molten that had been lurking beneath it pouring out.

"We could have been, you dumb idiot," I told the tiny Seph in my hands, as if he'd be able to hear me.

Once he'd collected himself he went on. "I'm not a complete pool of *vrakaash*," he said, chuckling darkly. "I've transferred everything I have here on Earth to you, Eva, since Mags isn't an adult yet. But it's for her, too. The house, my money, everything—all yours. I-I need you two to take care of yourselves, alright? I need to know that my mate and cub are out there safe, living their *best* lives. I want you to be able to go to school somewhere safe, Magdalena. I want you to pursue your passions. I want you to take some business classes and open that bakery, Eva. The universe needs your food." He swallowed, staring straight into the camera with an intensity I could feel tingling along my spine. "I miss you both already. I love you more than life itself, and I don't know that I can say sorry properly but it—it had to be done. You both carry my heart now so...so keep it safe." He stared forlornly at the camera some more, tears streaming down his unusually pale golden-brown face, before the video cut out. I flicked to the next picture, hoping for more, and saw a screenshot of a document somewhere on his phone with the title "logins". But I didn't need it. Not where I was going.

I locked the phone and slid it into my back pocket, wrapping my arms around my weeping child and cradling her against me. I rocked her, making soothing noises and rubbing her back. My heart ached for her, but my mind was already whirring with how to get him back, how to jump into the writhing river Styx and snatch his soul back to us, to where it belonged, not rotting away in some prison somewhere.

Eventually Maggie quieted, sniffling wetly, and pulled away to look at me with swollen eyes. I cupped her cheek, clucking in sympathy. "Why aren't you freaking out?" she asked in a rough croak.

"Because I have some ideas. I'm not going to let him do

this to us. To *himself*. I don't know if I can do anything but...I'm not going to let myself collapse until it's actually over."

"Fuck yeah, Mom," she breathed, grinning at me. Her eyes lit up, and she wiped at her face with the hem of her shirt. "You want to give him the 'ole dick twist when we get him back or can I do it?"

I laughed, pulling her in for a half-hug and a kiss on her temple. "You can do it. I'll kiss him silly so he knows we still love him."

"Gotcha; you hit him high, I hit him low."

We shared a shaky laugh, then I scooped the tablet off the stool and guided her back upstairs.

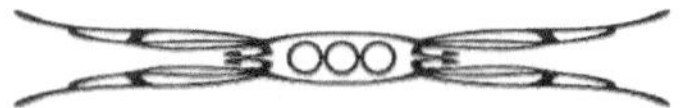

We didn't leave Seph's house until that night, once I'd been parked in front of that tablet, scrolling through endless nexus sites, combing through badly-translated information for the slightest hint of something that could help us. Maggie managed to find some food to microwave to keep us fed, allowing me to sink into myself and focus on doing All of the Research. My head felt like it was loose and light by the time the sun started setting again, but I had the beginnings of a plan.

I ushered my daughter out the door, snagging the keys to our fabulous new house, courtesy of Seph, who had somehow managed to put everything in our name, including his bank account, which had $716,000 in it. Phil had been blowing my phone up all day, but with so much money at my disposal and an honest-to-god crisis on my hands, I didn't have time for him.

With any luck, I'd never have to make time for him and that job ever again.

We drove home in silence, turning over the last 48 hours in our minds. A *lot* had happened, and it wasn't even over yet. I wanted to collapse into my bed and take several naps, but I couldn't rest. Not until I'd gotten Seph back. For how tired I was, I was also completely wired, desperate for him, for my mate. *God, that's so trippy*, I thought, almost laughing out loud. I was still getting used to the fact that soulmates were real, if rare, and that Sephyr Kasdaan, alien mercenary, was mine.

Once we'd made it back we split up, going to our respective rooms to pack a suitcase each. Starting tomorrow, things would be set in motion. Things that would hopefully lead him back into our lives without us getting hurt in the process.

You goddamn idiot, I sighed, watching the video he'd left for us for possibly the billionth time on mute. If only he'd trusted me more, or hell—if only he'd trusted *himself* more, then he'd still be with us and we'd be figuring it out together.

When I finally drifted asleep, my whole body wrung out and brittle, it was with Seph's phone cradled in my hand, his name a sigh on my lips.

Chapter 15

Un Otro Lonely Boy

<u>SEPHYR</u>

"C'mon, Kasdaan," the portly older billieuan sighed, trailing a finger down the trademark cleft that bisected his face vertically like all billieuans down to where his protective face mask started. Poor guys had a real nasty history with disease and wore protective gear anytime they stepped outside their houses. "You've gotta be able to give us more than that. Who was your contact on Earth? Where did you meet this Serr'eza? How did you manage to convince a th'rak to let in an outsider?" Detective Me'Sherra Be'Lin had been asking me this same litany of questions for what had to have been hours now, from the sour reek of the detective's sweat and how badly my ass was aching from sitting in this poor excuse for a chair.

Though compared to the aching in my chest, the angry throb of my tailbone and hips was nothing.

They'd had one request to make of me, *one thing* that they'd ever demanded of me, and like the sorry excuse for a male I was I hadn't been able to give it to them. My heart shred itself a little more behind my ribs, and I sucked in a breath to suppress the whine that wanted to slip out. "I've told you, detective. I had no contact on Earth—I *was* the contact. Serr'eza never met with me in person, it was always comms, and I've given you every record of that I still have. And *also* once again, I would like to go on record as saying I have no fucking clue why that *vrakaashaad* wanted an outside hire all of a sudden. His usual guy got himself killed and maybe he decided he wanted a fall guy this time around."

Detective Me'Sherra Be'Lin sighed again, turning shadowed, slowly swirling copper eyes on me. "I know that's what you've said, Mr. Kasdaan. But if I took a career criminal at his word I wouldn't be a very good detective, now would I?"

You're not a good detective anyway, you crusty old bastard, I thought viciously, just barely keeping my lip from curling in a sneer. He glared at me anyway, as if he could sense what I was thinking. He rolled his wrist, then gestured at me from across the table. "Start again from the beginning."

I gritted my teeth hard enough that I felt something creak. "Is that really necessary? I've already told you twice. I'm thirsty. And tired."

"Indulge me. Then maybe afterwards we can put you in a holding cell and get you some food and water."

I glared at the detective, certain that he wasn't allowed to withhold water from me, but I was too fucking exhausted to put up a fight. It had been a long day: after I hailed the Collective ship they scooped me up in my shuttle and jumped us to the nearest Collective outpost. All the while, every nerve in my body had been throbbing with the pain of loss, of having to deal with the fact that I'd lost Eva and Maggie forever. I'd never be able to see or even talk to the two most important beings in this whole universe ever again. The weight of that, the oppressive cold of it, was sapping any fight

I was finding almost as quickly as it sparked.

What was the point of fighting if I didn't have someone in my corner rooting for me, waiting for me? I was just some worthless pile of *vrakaash* without them.

I sighed, tipping my head back until it thunked against the chair back. "Fine, detective. You get one more before I start demanding a legal consul." I took a deep breath, every fiber of my being aching for the woman I'd left behind.

"I heard from a th'rak contact named Naran'haa that his boss—that would be Serr'eza—had a big job that he needed done in a hurry and if I did it my debts with them were all forgiven..." I recounted my conversations with Serr'eza, how he'd granted me the contract because Naran'haa vouched for me. I gave Detective Me'Sherra Be'Lin the contract details, then told them about my real plan to flee rather than participate in their slavery operation.

I didn't say a goddamn thing about Eva and Maggie. If the Collective knew I'd revealed myself to them, they might bring them into custody just to maintain the peace—the laws against contact with primitive worlds be damned. And I'd rather rot in prison the rest of my life than put them through that.

Once I'd finished my recounting of what had happened on Earth the detective grunted and pressed a button on a keyring strapped to his wrist, releasing my magcuffs from the chair and letting me stand. He sent a comm to someone else in the station, saying he was done with me and they could come grab me to take me to my cell. Then he ignored me until my escort arrived, picking lint from the furred tip of his tail as we sat in total silence. The guard, a young full-blooded yvrenii male with shrewd green eyes, took the controller from

Detective Me'Sherra Be'Lin and led me on a winding path through cold dim corridors until we reached a bay of holding cells. He led me to an empty one, then synced my magcuffs with the cell's security interface, keying my ID chip to the lock so that even if I got the cuffs off I wouldn't be able to get out; there were turrets outside the cells that would shoot unless an officer's ID was registered within six feet of mine.

"Sweet dreams, mutt," the officer spat, locking me in with a malicious grin. Fucking bigots just couldn't help kicking a male while he was down.

Then I was all alone in the ringing quiet, my thoughts and my loneliness swarming to the forefront, tearing strips of me from my bones one painful thought at a time. My whole body felt heavy, an ache that had nothing to do with physical exertion throbbing through me in time to my broken heart's pathetic beats. Every cell in me was crying out in protest of the light years between me and my mate, was demanding that I break out of here and return to her, and the fact that I couldn't, that I'd put myself here and was keeping this distance between us on purpose, might have actually been slowly killing me.

Now that I was alone I loosed the white-knuckled grip I'd been keeping on my despair, letting it flood me—*encouraging* it, even—begging the tears to come and sweep me away.

I managed to down a water tab and a nutri-bar from the dispenser on the wall before I lay down on my cot, my face to the wall so the cameras wouldn't pick up too much, and curled into a ball. I hugged myself tight as I cried, letting it all out as quietly as I could.

At some point, I slipped into a fitful sleep full of dreams where I searched and never found.

* * *

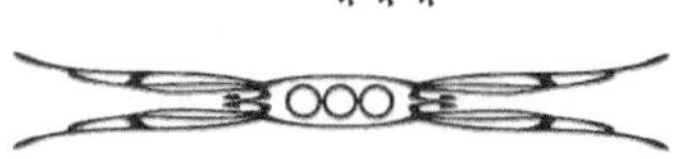

"Kasdaan, wake up!" A gruff voice barked, slamming something heavy into my door. I groaned, rolling over carefully so my swollen and aching head didn't roll right off my damn neck. I sat up, blinking blearily at the scowling officer on the other side of the viewing window. I squinted, bringing into focus the face of the young yvrenii who'd escorted me to my cell initially.

"Hurry up, you *vrakaashaad*, I have better things to do than babysit," he snarled, slamming his baton into the door again—no doubt that was what had woken me. I hauled myself to my feet, biting back more moans as my head throbbed and swam. I stopped at the line painted on the floor and the guard opened the door. My magcuffs snapped together, the ones on my ankle weighing my feet down so it would be harder for me to kick or run. Once the door was open he gestured me forward, and I followed him down the labyrinth of hallways to the same room—or one just like it— that I'd been talking to Detective Me'Sherra Be'Lin in before. I let a scowl settle onto my face, but kept my back straight and my chin up. I may have been a criminal, but I was still a person, and these assholes treating me like *vrakaash* was long past getting old.

The door swung open, revealing several people seated around the table this time: a new detective, this one myauanni, as well a felican in a sharp suit, and the two faces I was most desperate to see in the entire universe looking like they couldn't decide if they wanted to hit me or hug me.

Eva. Maggie.

My knees buckled, and with my wrists cuffed I couldn't catch my balance or stop my fall. I tipped back onto my ass, my short tail getting bumped *hard*—that was going to bruise badly.

"Seph!" Eva cried, standing and moving like she was going to try and come to me.

I wanted to say something, to tell her to get out of here, to ask her what was going on, to beg for her forgiveness and tell her I loved her more than anything, but all that came out was a confused garble. "What's wrong? Are you ill? What the fuck did you assholes *do* to him?" she cried as she struggled against the hold the yvrenii officer had on her. Seeing that, I snapped, surging to my feet and snarling at that pissy little asshole. He was bigger than me, being full-blooded yvrenii, but that had never stopped me before. Hadn't ever saved anyone from a beatdown before, either.

"Release Ms. Nadzija, Officer Gricht," the felican female snapped. "As we've already disclosed, we are dealing with a true mate bond, here." That cooled my anger a touch, snapping my eyes to my mate. Released from the hold Officer Gricht—a name I was going to make sure I remembered— had had on her, she flung herself the rest of the way over to me, wrapping her arms tight around my neck. I couldn't separate my arms, being cuffed, but I buried my face in her hair, pressing into her throat and breathing her sweet scent into my starving lungs. I couldn't stop tears of relief from trickling from my gritty eyes at the wave of sublime relief that swept through me at having my other half returned to me.

"What are you doing here, babygirl?" I breathed. "Am I still asleep?"

She snorted, pulling back to look at me, tears glistening in those endless stormcloud eyes of hers. "We're here to bring you home, you jackass." She cupped my face, staring deep into my eyes. "I missed you so damn much. I'm so glad you're alright." She looked down at my hands, seeming to realize for the first time I was still cuffed. Her eyes went cold and furious. *"Why is my mate handcuffed?"* she asked the room at large in a voice that was pure venom, turning slowly to face the officers in the room. I couldn't tell you why, but seeing her fury unleashed was making heat pool low in my belly, my dick twitching against my leg and my sleeve clenching.

Fuck, she was so hot.

"Has Mr. Kasdaan been hostile in your...care?" the felican asked, pulling a tablet out of a sleek leather briefcase.

"No," the myauanni detective answered with a sigh. "But Kasdaan is a known criminal, Mx. Yennya," Ah, so not a female, then, I corrected myself silently, "and it is standard procedure—"

"What crime has Mr. Kasdaan been charged with, Sergeant Tuli?" the felican interrupted smoothly, pulling up several documents on their tablet.

"Well, it's not about *current* crimes, Mx. Yennya—"

"So, he hasn't been charged? You're holding him under false pretenses?"

The myauanni sergeant bristled, his tail puffing in irritation. But he didn't say anything.

It felt like I was missing something, like I'd blinked and a vital piece of information had slipped right by me. What was all this about charges? I'd broken the law—often and thoroughly—and that was that...wasn't it?

"He was in restricted space, by his own admission," Officer Gricht chimed in, looking furious. "That's prison time right there."

Sergeant Tuli held up a hand to silence the furious yvrenii. "That's enough, Gricht." He pulled out his keyring and flipped through the remotes attached to it until he'd found the one he wanted, and pressed a yellow button on its face. Within seconds my magcuffs had deactivated and clattered to the floor. "You're free to go, Mr. Kasdaan."

I blinked, my eyes darting between everyone in the room. I'd definitely missed something huge. What had Eva and Maggie done? How had they managed to convince the Collective to just let me walk free? My headache kept getting worse and worse with each attempt to understand.

I was still trying to process those words, that I was free, when Eva threaded her arm through mine and tugged me after her and the legal counselor, Mx. Yennya. I was *still* trying to process—and still failing—while they led us through the precinct and out into the garage, where a sleek black hover was parked near the entrance.

Once we were inside and strapped in, I sagged back into the plush seats, looking at my family in disbelief. "What...what just happened?" I managed to ask, dazed.

Maggie leaned forward and punched me in the chest, making me collapse forward and wheeze. "That's for breaking your promise and making Mom cry," she snarled, tears coursing down her cheeks. Then she lunged at me and threw her arms around my neck, squeezing me tight. "I'm glad you're back, Seph."

"Magdalena, we had agreed to a metaphorical punching," Eva sighed, rubbing her daughter's back and wincing at me. I just smiled, my hand joining Eva's in soothing our cub.

"It's alright, I deserved it. And then some." I eased Maggie back into her seat and took both of their hands, my eyes sliding to the floor of the hover while I struggled to find the courage to let the words out that were clangoring in my throat. *I'm sorry. I shouldn't have done it. I love you both so much. I've been miserable without you. Eva, being apart from you was the worst pain I've ever felt.* But all that came out was another "I deserved it," whispered to the floor.

"No, you didn't," Maggie admitted. "I'm sorry I hit you, Seph. That wasn't right." I blinked up at her, surprised.

"Of course it was. I hurt you, you hurt me. That's how it works."

"Oh, Lord, Mom, he's got so much baggage. Jesus get this man to therapy *now*."

I bristled, getting defensive. "What do you mean by baggage? Why do I need to go see an emoreg?"

Eva shot a stern look at her daughter and turned to me, her eyes softening. "You've had a hard life, Sephyr. You couldn't help it, you did the best you could, but I think it's safe to say that it...affected things for you. Things like how you see situations and what sorts of things you think need to be communicated to the people who care about you. When you're ready I think it'll help you to sort through that. Don't you?"

I swallowed my angry words. She may have had a point.

I frowned, eyes still locked on the floor, and she made a little noise of distress. "Hey, what's going on in there, Seph?" I clenched my teeth, jaw ticking, and she combed her fingers carefully through the tangled curls of my hair.

"Are you...regretting the mate bond?" I asked, my voice so shamefully small and quiet in the hover's cab.

"What? No, of course not!" she cried, rearing back as if I'd struck her. "I'm frustrated with you, but I still love you, I still want you. Of *course* I do." Her fingers threaded through mine, squeezing tight, and the gash that had been ripping through my chest shrank. There was nothing but truth in her wide gray eyes.

I swallowed. Maybe they were right about my seeing an emoreg…but it was something I'd have to warm up to. "Okay." I closed my eyes, taking a shaky breath. "If you're not tossing me out on my ass then I'd like to know what in Veldar's creation is going on."

Eva sighed, putting her arm around my shoulders and squeezing. "Well, big guy, I guess I do have a lot to fill you in on. We've been busy while you've been locked up.

"So; I did some digging on the nexus once we realized you were gone and discovered that mates are indeed protected under several treaties. But what I *also* found was that there's a whole department in the Collective's enforcement division that's trying to take down the th'rak slave rings. Three orbits ago—I think that's years?—they passed a memorandum that offers amnesty to anyone who reports valuable intel concerning those groups. There's a lot of strings attached, but you absolutely qualify for that deal; you just didn't know it, and those assholes used that against you."

"Yeah, that's why you don't just run off in the middle of the night, my dude," Maggie added, lightly punching my arm on my other side. "We could have found all of that together and saved ourselves a trip."

"Well, not entirely," Eva chimed in, her hands roving over my arms, squeezing my hand, as if she couldn't stop checking to make sure that I was really there, that I was fine. "We can't stay on Earth, but they can't split us up, so they offered to relocate us. I couldn't remember where you said were from but they said you have an aunt currently residing on Billieu —"

"Wait, wait. No, that can't be right. When I came of age they told me I had no family left." My heart started thundering in my ears. It couldn't possibly be true...could it?

"I had them send the info to your tablet, so you can take a peek once this is all done. All that really matters is we got you out of there, and we get to stay together. Just like we hoped."

I threw myself into her embrace, pressing my face into her throat. "How did you do all this?" I breathed, holding her tight. "You are a *miracle*, love."

She chuckled, holding me and pressing soft kisses into my hair. Something in my chest melted at that. "It wasn't any harder than having to deal with insurance companies all day. They weren't happy that a human was reaching out to them, but when I explained about us being mates and showed them the blood test results and explained that you were trying to give them information on a th'rak slaving ring they got a lot less pissy." I snorted. If that had been them being *less* pissy then they must have been something else for her to deal with.

But she had. Alone, until she'd found the consul currently driving us away from the outpost station, the dampening field thoughtfully engaged between the cab and the back. Even with her anxiety, with a child to take care of, she'd taken all that on and gotten my dumb ass out of there.

"Fuck, I love you so much," I rasped, cupping her face in my trembling hands and pulling her close for a kiss.

When her lips crashed into mine we both sucked in a breath, her fingers burrowing into my hair as we did our damnedest to coax our flesh to melt together, for the lines between our bodies to disappear and let our souls finish the merge they'd already started.

Maggie made a dramatic gagging sound. "You guys are so nasty, oh my god."

I pulled away a little and licked across Eva's lips like an animal, trailing my tongue along her jaw, making Maggie squeal and throw something at me that stung a little when it hit my bicep. Eva yanked away, rubbing at the slobber I'd left on her face and laughing.

It was so goddamn good to be back.

Chapter 16

Relocating

<u>EVA</u>

A cool thing about aliens was that they were able to get my name right; they were so used to having to pronounce things from all different corners of the galaxy that "Nadzija" didn't give them any real problems.

But in a lot of other ways, they were entirely too like humans.

"There's got to be a better way to do this," I whispered to Seph, my now-legally-recognized mate.

He grinned, shaking his head. "Guaranteed, babygirl. But this is the way they're doing it." He put a big warm hand on my knee, crinkling the paper gown I was wearing, the twin to his own. "You doing alright?"

I nodded, my foot jiggling. I didn't like doctor's offices, but overall it hadn't been too bad so far. Mostly I was bored and impatient to get on with my day. "Does Billieu really need this much information about our health before we can move here?"

He nodded, pressing his full mouth into a line. "Yeah, these poor guys had it rough for a really long time. Back to back pandemics that spread like crazy and decimated their population. They've had to be real careful to keep afloat, and part of it is doing all these health checks. I think the history lesson we got at the immigration office was really truncated. I remember there being a lot more to it when I learned about it in school."

I pouted and crossed my arms, but when he put it like that I couldn't really get mad at them. Even if it had been literally hours since we'd first arrived here.

We'd decided to settle on Billieu so that Seph would have the option of finding and meeting his newly-discovered aunt if he decided he wanted to. And I rather liked the look of Billieu aside from that: it was a small but beautiful little planet, with busy urban centers that didn't fight against nature like so many human cities did back on Earth. Instead, they nurtured it and existed *with* it. There was also a thriving art scene here that I was hoping Maggie could get involved in so she could blossom as an artist. And Sephyr had made sure I knew that there were plenty of programs that helped people set up businesses. He was determined to see me open up a bakery, the goof.

But the thing was, after everything that had happened, it was kind of really doable. The information Seph had provided to the Collective had led to arrests, and as part of the deal Mx. Yennya had organized we got a nice little payout of 10,000 credits for each lead that panned out. And thanks to Seph they'd nabbed Serr'eza, Naran'haa, Siit'ron, *and* several other high-ranking members of the brotherhood Sephyr hadn't ever met. All told we walked away with just under 70k, along with the satisfaction of knowing that so many people were safer now that those guys were locked up.

And Billieu wasn't just progressive for its views on the environment; we'd been told that all citizens, even immigrants, qualified for aid which meant we never had to worry about being homeless or hungry. It was why the art scene was so robust here; people had the mental and emotional bandwidth to just create, their basic needs met no matter what.

It was so beautiful, and anytime I thought too much about it I wanted to cry.

There was a soft chime overhead, interrupting my train of thought, and a little yellow light lit up over the door.

"Enter," Seph called out, and an older yvrenii female with silver-streaked black hair and impressive tusks strode in with a warm smile.

"Hello, there. Welcome to Billieu, Mr. Kasdaan, Ms. Nadzija. How would you like to be addressed?"

"Oh, I'm Eva."

"Seph is fine."

"And pronoun preferences?" she asked, making notes on a tablet she had cradled in the crook of her elbow.

"She/her," I responded.

"He/him," Seph added, and the doctor made those notes as well.

"Excellent!" she trilled. Three green-brown eyes looked over at us from behind gleaming spectacles. "I'm Dr. Ritelak, she/her as well. How are you two doing today?" The warm older female chatted with us for a bit and went over our test results in a general sense. She revealed that I was only the second human she'd ever treated, while Seph was the first yvrenii/felican bi-special person she'd treated.

"Which is actually at the heart of what I need to talk to

you two about next," Dr. Ritelak said, her expression dimming and her eyes going grave. "I know you two are true mates—and congratulations on that, by the way—but there is a...complication present that you'll need to be aware of..." Seph pulled me in close, draping one arm over my paper-clad shoulders and grasping my hand tight with the other. "Do you know about hybrid sterility?" she continued. Both me and Seph shook our heads.

Dr. Ritelak took a deep breath. "It's not common for inter-species couples to produce offspring. The sex cells just aren't capable of combining and dividing properly. But every now and again it'll happen, most commonly among true mate pairs where unamarin is released by both parents. We think it aids in the ability of the sex cells to make that initial combination that will lead to an embryo.

"That's how we have people like you, Mr. Kasdaan. But while there is the occasional child born to interspecies couples, that child is going to be unable to conceive themself. That's hybrid sterility. Which means that if you were hoping to have more children together it would have to be through donors or adoption."

I blinked, surprised but not devastated. I hadn't wanted to get pregnant again anyway—but I hadn't considered whether or not Seph would want kids. I turned to look at my mate, to see how he felt, and was surprised to see he was looking...relieved?

"So nothing's wrong with Eva? She's not sick?"

Dr. Ritelak's serious expression eased, and she smiled at us gently. "No, you're both perfectly healthy otherwise. As is your daughter, Ms. Nadzija."

I sagged into Seph, tension I hadn't even been aware of

leaving me in a rush. "Oh, thank you, that's so good to hear!" I put my hand to my chest and loosed a sigh. "Oh, that reminds me—she'll need a referral to an endocrinologist for her hormone replacement therapy. Who would I go to to secure that?"

Dr. Ritelak's brows furrowed, making her top eye squint. "Referral? I'm afraid I don't know that term."

"Um..." I tried to think of another word. "Well, back on Earth there was a general doctor, and then specialists would take care of more specific parts of the body. But you can't just *see* them, you'd need your main doctor to refer you to them—"

"You won't need referrals here, love," Seph chimed in. "She can get that all from her main doctor."

I blinked again. "Really?" Okay, so maybe these aliens had things more figured out than I'd realized.

Seph grinned, showing off his fangs. "Yep."

I reached up and cupped his face. "How do you feel about...what we just learned? Are you...okay?"

His grin dropped a fraction of a watt, but his eyes remained calm and serene. "I'm a little disappointed, but it's never been something I thought I'd get to do. Be a parent. But here we are with Maggie, and she's a handful all on her own." He kissed my temple, rubbing his cheek on the top of my head in a fairly catlike show of affection. "I don't have any issues with adopting if we want more, though. I might even...prefer that. It would be a chance to do for someone else what no one had done for me. Get a kid out of the system. Love them." He said it so softly it ripped my heart right out of my chest. I leaned in and gave him a kiss on his stubbly cheek.

"I'd love to do that with you."

"You two are very sweet," Dr. Ritelak said, gently coaxing us back on track with what she had wanted to tell us. Once she'd finished imparting everything she signed off on our immigration medical forms and sent us on our way.

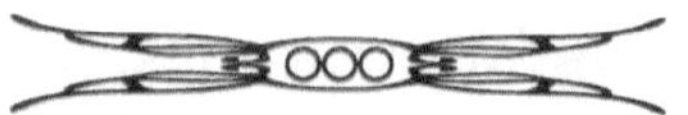

<u>SEPHYR</u>

<u>FOUR MONTHS LATER</u>

I was regretting everything about this, my heart pounding so hard it felt like it was making my whole body pulse. My stomach was churning, acid flirting with the back of my throat and making me swallow. Why was I so goddamn nervous? I didn't even *know* this female. She was a total stranger to me. All I knew was that she was my dad's sister, also mated to a felican, funnily enough, and had been in the yvrenii vanguard until I was 20, unable to adopt me. But why hadn't she ever sought me out? Why not try and find me, or at least talk to me?

I'd debated for weeks, then months, about how I should go about this, if I even *should* do this. I mean, I'd made it this far without her, so why make it a big deal now?

But between talking it through with Eva and my new emoreg, Dr. Shiya, I'd realized I had to for myself. So I could look the only blood I had left in all the universe in the eyes and ask her why. Why hadn't she tried to find me? Why had she abandoned me? Why didn't she care about me?

Why didn't she *love* me?

And I needed to see her face when I asked her. So I hadn't reached out over comms. Hadn't messaged her at all—I'd just packed my little family into our hover so I knew I'd have support if it went badly, and drove us all over here. To the address Eva had been given all those months ago.

I sucked in a breath through my nose and let it sigh out of my mouth. Then I did it again, and again, until I felt calm enough to ring the entry bell. I pressed the little button, heart in my throat, and after a few seconds a breathy female voice called out through the comm, "Yes? Can I help you?"

"My name's Sephyr. I'm looking for...Uraka."

"Oh. I'll go get her, then! Just a moment." The comm clicked off and I shoved my hands in my pockets, looking over my shoulder at my two beautiful females, tucked safely in the back of the hover and giving me encouraging smiles and thumbs-up. I knew Eva was balancing a box of her "exotic" Earth muffins on her lap, the cardboard emblazoned with her bakery's name, Earth to Billieu Confections, along the side—just in case it went *well*. I smiled back at them, fluttering my fingers in a wave, then blew Eva a kiss, making her flush. I loved that I had that effect on her.

I had expected Uraka to pick up the comm and talk to me through that first, but instead, the front door swung open with a huff, and a scowling yvrenii female with light brown hair and the same golden eyes I'd inherited from my dad filled the doorway. The delicate swirling characters of an yvrenii mate tattoo spidered over one of her cheeks, making my own face feel suddenly bare. Should I have gotten them, too?

As soon as she saw me her olive green skin paled, and she sagged sideways against the door. "Urin?" she asked faintly, and I couldn't help the half step forward I took to try and catch her if she fell. She blinked hard, shaking her head, and then her expression shifted. "No, sorry, of course not. My mate has told me your name is...Sephyr?"

I swallowed, my throat so tight I didn't know if I'd be able to work words past it. "Yeah," I croaked. "Um, here's the thing. Urin Kasdaan was my dad. I'm your nephew."

Uraka did sag then, and I rushed forward to catch her and ease her to the ground. She clutched at me, her three eyes locked on my face in disbelief. Her main eyes were growing shiny with tears. "Urin...had a son?" she asked, so quietly I almost didn't hear her.

Something broke open in me then, bringing tears to my own eyes. She hadn't known. She'd had no clue that I existed, hadn't even known that her brother had had a youngling.

Distantly, I heard the doors of a hover open and shut behind me, thought I might have heard Eva calling my name across a great distance, but my world had shrunk down to the solid wall of muscle clutching me tight to her breast, rocking me and sobbing my name and my father's name, thanking Veldar in the mother tongue.

Eva called my name again, this time from right behind me, and I snapped out of my stupor, wrestling myself free from Uraka's incredibly strong grip. "I'm fine, love," I reassured my mate, getting to my feet and taking her hand.

Uraka also got up, beaming wide at Eva and Maggie. "And who is this, blood of my blood? A mate and youngling?"

I nodded, my chest puffing out with pride. "Yeah. This is my mate, Eva, and our cub Maggie." Maggie waved shyly but stayed quiet, watching Uraka warily.

"How glorious!" she boomed, smiling warmly. "May I hug you both? I have been told it is better to ask, even when they are family. My human friend Joss says that there is much variability in how often your peoples express physical affection."

Eva blinked in surprise, but recovered herself quickly and held her arms open. "Of course, thank you for asking." Uraka swept her up into a big bear hug that pulled Eva off her feet with a squeak. Uraka released her, then turned to Maggie.

"Um, no thanks," Maggie said, but held out her hand. "But it's um, it's nice to meet you." My aunt smiled warmly, taking her much smaller hand gently and shaking it.

"It is nice to meet you too, little one. Please, both of you, come in and meet my mate, Djelani."

Eva hung back with me as we followed Uraka into her apartment to meet her felican mate. "So it went well? What did she say?"

I took her hand. "She didn't know about me. She had no clue my dad had even had a child."

My mate shot me a commiserating look. "I wonder what happened there? But at least you're getting a chance to know her now. And obviously it's still early but...I like her. She seems like a hoot."

A hoot? I was never going to get used to English. "I like her, too," I admitted as she showed Maggie a lasknife that was as long as my daughter's arm.

It struck me then just how much had changed. This time last year I was lost, desperate for a place to belong but completely in denial about it. And now I was standing in my aunt's apartment, my incredible mate in my arms and our child showing my aunt's mate pictures of her latest sculpture. I was in school, getting certified to become a social worker for kids in the foster system here on Billieu. My dream was to eventually go back to Exodia and do what I could to help there.

I tightened my arms around Eva, leaning over to kiss her

temple before going over to Uraka and Djelani to get to know them better.

Life was good.

Epilogue

EVA

"Magdalena, your date is here!"

I heard a furious screech come from inside Maggie's room, the door's comm buzzing to life a moment later. "Mom, you said you'd be cool!"

I pressed my lips into a line, holding back a laugh I knew she wouldn't appreciate. "Is this not me being cool?" I responded, winking at Sephyr, my gorgeous mate, as he went to let in the young yvrenii male here to take my daughter on her first date.

"You know it's not!" Her door slid open, revealing her artfully mussed teal hair and half-done eyeliner. "Your tone is all 'oh my god this is so cute, your little boyfriend, hu hu hu'."

I laughed, stealing a kiss on the cheek. "Well it *is* cute. Krett sounds like a very nice young man and I only get to see my daughter go on her first date once—"

"We only have our courting permits! It's barely anything!" She spun back around and shooed me away with a flap of her hand. "I have to finish putting on my makeup; I *cannot* deal with you being weird right now."

I pretended to be hurt, then slipped down the hallway to join Seph and our guest.

When he'd officially adopted Maggie, he'd fallen right into the overprotective father role, and I flinched internally when I realized that was what was currently unfolding in my living room.

"What clubs are you in, Krett?" my mate was asking, his smile easy but his eyes promising that there *were* wrong answers. "What do you get up to after school?"

"Hey, guys!" I trilled, sliding in next to Seph and giving Krett—who was literally sweating behind his thick three-lens glasses—the biggest and warmest smile I could. "Mags is just finishing up getting ready, hun," I told him, grabbing Seph's knee and squeezing it in warning. "Can we get you anything to eat? Drink?"

"Um—" Krett sputtered and coughed behind his surgical-style mask. We'd decided to stay on Billieu until Maggie was done with the alien equivalent of high school. We'd been dealing with PPE for so long that I hardly registered it anymore. "W-water. If it's not too much, um, trouble," the poor guy finally managed.

I squeezed Seph's knee again and he got to his feet with a sigh, heading for our modest kitchen. "Be right back."

Once my mate was out of the room I turned to Krett and gave him another smile. "Sorry about him," I said, wincing. "He's very protective of me and Maggie and he doesn't always know what to do with those feelings. I promise you though that as long as you treat our girl right you have nothing to worry about."

Krett's throat worked in a swallow. "He said if I hurt her he'd kill me," he confided in a tense whisper. "Did he…mean that?"

I kept my smile plastered on my face. "No! Of course not!" But I'd hesitated for just a second, and I think he'd caught it. Seph *probably* wouldn't resort to murder...but I couldn't honestly say it was impossible. "So how did you and Maggie meet, again?" I blurted, desperate to change the subject. I knew already, of course, since Maggie had told both of us several times all about Krett and how he'd offered to tutor her in their math class, proving much gentler and quieter than one would expect nearly seven feet of heavily muscled yvrenii male to be. She'd been immediately smitten by his shy sweetness and strange sense of humor, and when she'd finally admitted her feelings she'd been still more smitten by his admission that he'd loved her from afar for a long time, and had taken the opportunity to offer his services as a way to get to know her better.

It was absolutely the cutest thing I'd ever heard, and I really hoped it would work out for them. But it all started tonight, with Seph *not* biting Krett's head off and scaring him away. "He means hurt her in a bad way," I murmured after Krett had given his own version of events, blushing and stammering adorably the whole time. I heard Seph's footsteps padding back towards us. "He understands that young people are going to hurt each other on accident, especially when it's their first relationship." Seph reappeared, handing Krett one of the sterile water pouches we kept around for guests; Billieu really did take sanitation very seriously. "But taking advantage, putting your hands on her inappropriately...those are the kinds of things we want to protect her from. And I don't think you're that kind of person, right?"

Krett looked disgusted, even with his mask obscuring so much of his face. "No, not at all, ma'am," he assured me, shooting a pleading look at Seph, too. "I—I really care about Magdalena. I'd never—"

"I know, hun. Thank you for putting our minds at ease." I shot a look at Seph, daring him to start up again with the third degree, but he looked mollified.

"Sorry about that," he mumbled, twisting his lips. "Just want to make sure my cub is well taken care of."

Krett nodded, tearing open the pouch and slipping the straw that extended into the port on his mask designed for it. "I get it," he said, his voice unexpectedly quiet. "I know…I know how I look."

Seph stiffened. "It's got nothing to do with how you look, kid," he said gently, leaning forward. "I'm sorry I made you feel that way. I just, uh…I gotta learn to relax, I guess. I'm half yvrenii myself, you know."

The young male straightened from the hunch he'd settled into. "Really? I guess that makes sense, with the third eye."

Seph grinned, flashing his fangs and making his tusks stand out a little more. "Yeah, my pa was. And my aunt used to be in the vanguard. Retired now, though. I look more like my felican mom at a glance so most people don't realize right away." He turned to me, looking at my face with tender love and wonder. "You're so much better at this sort of thing than I am, babygirl. Maybe next time you answer the door and I go get Mags."

I laughed, leaning into him. "But if you don't practice then how will you get better?"

He groaned. "*Vrakaash*, you sound like Dr. Shiya."

Maggie swept into the room just then looking like an emo

princess, putting a blessed end to the awkward moment. She looked so beautiful and grown up it took my breath away. It was amazing what two years on Billieu had done for her; getting away from all of Earth's bullies had been wonderful, but the level of gender-affirming care she'd been able to get here had completely transformed her spirit and had allowed her to feel so much more comfortable and confident in her skin.

I glanced at Krett, his eyes wide and filled with so much wonder and awe I wanted to cry. He watched her closely, like she was a thing of dreams and he was worried she'd disappear if he so much as blinked. There was no way we had anything to worry about.

"Oh my god, are you *crying?*" Maggie cried, looking past me at Seph. I turned to look at my mate, and sure enough, tears sparked along his lashes, threatening to fall.

"Shut up, you are," he said, wiping his eyes. But he stood and wrapped her up in a tight but brief hug. "You look beautiful, monkey," I heard him say quietly.

I thought I detected a quiet sniffle in turn, but when Maggie pulled away she didn't look teary-eyed. "Dork."

She turned to Krett, smiling shyly, then handed him a small figure I'd seen her sculpting all week. "I uh...I made this. Thought you might like it so—so you can have it. If you want."

He stood, dwarfing her 5'8" frame but taking the little figure—a yessen, catlike creatures commonly kept as pets here on Billieu, curled up in sleep—with aching tenderness. "You made this for me?" he asked, stroking the tiny face with a reverent claw. "It's incredible. I—thank you. So much."

I stood and joined Seph, looping my arm through his and

tucking myself close into his side. "I need to get a picture of you two!" I announced, snagging my tablet from the coffee table and quickly pulling up the camera app.

"Mom!"

"Oh, hush—let me have this, insolent child! One picture and then you're free to go. Please?"

She loosed a long-suffering sigh, then looked shyly up at her date and tucked a lock of teal hair behind her heavily-pierced ear. Blushing furiously, they put their arms around each other and turned to me, smiling politely when I told them to. Then Maggie was swanning down the hall, dragging a startled Krett behind her. She snagged a mask of her own from the dispenser by the door and called a hasty goodbye before slipping out the door and running away.

"Young love," Seph sighed, turning to me and stooping to pick me up in a bridal carry. I squeaked, wrapping my arms around his neck on instinct. "That kid's more of a gentleman than I've ever been in my life. Maggie will be fine with him."

"Then what was with that interrogation?!" I sputtered, flicking the tip of his ear.

"It's called an insurance policy, love," he growled, nipping at my fingers when I tried to boop his nose.

"He just about shit his pants, Seph."

He hummed. "But he *didn't*." He stopped, and I realized we were in our bedroom, his shins pressed right up to the side of the bed. He tossed me onto the comforter, making me squawk in outrage. He jumped on after me, caging me in with his body, pressing me into the mattress with his weight in a way that made me breathless. He dipped his head, sweeping me up into a heated kiss that sent need rushing straight to my core.

His knee wedged itself between my legs, pressing into my clit and making me whimper. I started fumbling at his clothes, needing him bare, needing *me* bare, needing to feel my mate deep inside me more than I needed my next breath.

I kept waiting for the bond to get less intense, for me to be able to be in the same room as Seph and not need to touch him, to hold him, but after more than two years together it was still as intense as it had ever been.

He broke the kiss to rip his shirt off over his head, flinging it into a corner of the room and then shoving my own shirt up roughly and coaxing that off, too. He kissed and licked along my collarbone, making me shiver, then slipped the cups of my bra down to bare my breasts to his hungry mouth. "Don't *you* look good enough to eat," he growled, latching onto one nipple and laving it with his tongue. After just a few swipes I was panting and mewling, arching up into him in a silent plea for more. He opened his mouth wide, like he intended to take a bite out of me, letting his fangs and tusks scrape deliciously over my sensitive flesh. I cried out, my hands gripping the side of his head as he tilted it in a different direction and did it again.

He switched sides, bracing on one elbow while the other slithered between us to undo our pants. His leg was still pressed tight into the apex of my thighs, and I was grinding against him shamelessly, wound up so tight already that I could feel the first shivers of an impending orgasm.

Seph released me, rolling to the side to finish undressing and helping me out of my own clothes. "No Maggie means you can scream as loud as you want to, gorgeous," he smirked, sliding down my body until he was between my legs, spreading me wide for his appreciative three-eyed gaze.

"So let's make you sing tonight, hmm?"

It was no idle threat; he worked me like a man possessed, tonguing and sucking me until I came against his mouth over and over and over again; after five I stopped counting. The sheets were soaked under my ass, my body boneless and dripping with sweat and my throat raw from the screams he'd wrung out of me—as promised—when he finally peeled himself off of me with a self-satisfied smirk to sink his thick length into me.

I was so sensitized, so worked up, that I was coming again after just a few strokes, keening my pleasure into the crook of his neck while he continued to pump into me, crooning soft words into my ear as he kissed and nibbled at my throat. It wasn't too much longer before his rhythm was stuttering, his spine snapping straight as his face contorted with pleasure and my name ripped itself from his throat, a prayer and a curse all at once. He held me tight as he emptied himself into me, and now it was my turn to murmur gently, to tell him he'd done so well and that he was so beautiful when he came. He shuddered, thrusting one last time, before letting out a deep sigh and rolling us over onto our sides, our bodies still connected.

"We should encourage Maggie to go out with Krett more," I mused dreamily, my body loose and sated. He chuckled, kissing me sweetly, almost gently.

"We should just rent her her own apartment. Kick the baby bird out of the nest so I can take my mate on every surface that's even remotely stable in this place."

A thrill shot through me at the idea. But— "She's only sixteen," I reminded him. "And she'll leave when she's ready. So you'll just have to be fine with doing a little sneaking…"

His golden eyes flashed, full lips quirking up on one side in a wicked grin. "I can do that," he rasped, cupping the back of my head in his hand and pulling me in for another kiss. "I can do whatever you want, gorgeous. You got me wrapped around that little finger of yours."

I smiled, returning his kiss eagerly. "I have the best mate in the whole universe. I love you, Seph," I told him.

"I love you, too, Eva. Always and forever."

Well, well, well, if it isn't my favorite people ;3 Hey, readers!

Hope Like Hell has had at least five names over the course of its development, but I got there eventually! I had wanted to do something loosely based off of *Spy X Family*, but with some of the vibes of the *Aliens Among Us* series by Tiffany Roberts, but then it took on a life of its own and now we're here.

I love talking about the "fun facts" in these things because, as you'll know if you follow me on my socials, I'm autistic and info-dumping is one of my love languages uwu

So: fun fact the first is that Eva and Maggie's last name, Nadzija, is the Polish word for "hope" (I really should have picked up on the whole "put hope in the title" thing sooner but I'm a bit of a dummy sometimes—it's kind of my thing).

Fun fact number two (and if you speak a Latinate language you might have already picked up on this one): Serr'eza is someone we've seen before, as are his lieutenants Siit'ron and Naran'haa. That's right, I done did it: I put Cherry, Orange, and Lemon in here as the bad guys—again. But this time they get sold out and eventually imprisoned. I'm a very squishy softie and having them get away in *All or*

Nothing bothered me, so when I was brainstorming why Sephyr would be on Earth it came to me that who better than our three least favorite th'rak slavers to be the catalyst? And because I am a *huge* dork, their real names are based on either the Spanish or French words for the nicknames Joss gives them in AoN: Ceresa is cherry in Spanish, Naranja is orange (also in Spanish), and Citron is Lemon in French.

I'll see myself out.

Final cameo from a character we've seen before is a super subtle one: Sephyr and Xollen are seeing the same emoreg/therapist, Dr. Shiya Vakkas. LOL.

I also keep calling my MMCs "El Lonely Boy" when they're alone and sad about it and this is the most random reference to a thing I can't even honestly say I'm super into; you remember that band that had some hits in the 90's/00's, Los Lonely Boys? Yeah somehow that's a thing for me. Just the band *name*, not even necessarily the music. I can't explain it, but felt the need to explain myself.

Fun fact number three is that if you read this and thought "man, it sure does seem like Eva and Maggie have a touch of the 'tism"—you're right! I started this one shortly before my diagnosis, and when I picked it back up several months after it struck me that there were a lot of points where I'd written them that way on accident. So I just edited it to be more intentional but kept the characters themselves unaware. You don't need a diagnosis to tell you what you already know, and all mine really did was give me the ability to point to a thing and say "no, look—I *need* this accommodation, you twatwaffle."

In addition to geeking out, I also like to address the more sensitive topics that come up in my books in these notes, so that you can get a sense of where I'm coming from with this stuff. And making Maggie trans, only to get bullied, was something that I really wrestled with. I never want my characters to go through anything hard or painful (*cannot* emphasize how squishy I am enough), but Maggie is based off of someone very near and dear to me in my life, and bullying is tragically common for anyone who gets labeled "other". The person Maggie's based on never had this specific thing happen to them, but I heard it threatened to them at one point by someone at a party we were both attending. At the time I wasn't in any sort of position to get them out of that environment, so (and I admit this may be selfish) writing Maggie getting help and support was a kind of catharsis, maybe even wish fulfillment. My loved one is doing much better now, but it breaks my heart when they confide the depression and anxiety they still deal with, how the microaggressions of the world weigh them down and hurt them, and so I tried to put a little trans joy into the end of this one, as a sort of wish that this person in my life will someday get that level of happiness and acceptance, too.

Another personal element in this story is the fact that Eva has hidradenitis supporitiva. It's something I've struggled with since it first showed its ugly mug around when I was 10, when I started going through puberty. DO NOT Google it with Safe Search off because it *does* most commonly appear around the genitals and NSFW areas, but it isn't an STI. I thought it was for the longest time, despite it cropping up almost a decade before I would become sexually active (yes, I was a bit of a late bloomer). But it's autoimmune, and believed to be a chronic infection of subcutaneous (i.e., beneath the layers of the skin) sweat glands that results in boils and cysts. It's gory, it's painful, and it really does do a number on the 'ole self-esteem. I was told time and again by my mother that it was because I wasn't cleaning myself right, that it was because of my poor diet, my clothing choices, etc.—and while those things can factor into the severity of the outbreaks, at the end of the day it's just something misfiring in my body. So if you have it, and someone is trying to tell you those things, spit right in their stupid face and tell them to eat a butt because that ain't it. I can guarantee you're doing your best with the little bit of information out there, and that's all you can do in these situations. You got this, fellow HS warriors <3

Aside from that, some updates usually wind up in these rambling monstrosities. So:

1) Out of the Dark, the sequel to ALITD, is getting picked at, if slowly. I had to course-correct and restart and then I got distracted getting this guy out of the doom corner to publish and it's been set aside for now.

2) Me and Carlotta Hughes are cooking up a series of short, fun shifter romances set, at least initially, in Canada. We're calling it Mount Maple Shifters and it is silly, goofy, *and* ridiculous—buckle up and prepare your body for non-stop puns. Particularly about moose, because oh, yeah—they're going to feature moose shifters XD

3) The brain goblins are starting to sprinkle ideas for Uraka and Djelani's book into my brain meats, but before I dive into it I want to finish OotD, MMS, and a couple of shorts. So for those of you who are desperate for more Ura trust me I am *right there with you* and that is a big part of why she shows up at the end as Seph's long-lost aunt.

4) My website is live! MirandaSapphireWrites.com is up and running—but it's not quite finished yet. My husband had

to take care of some important life stuff and put the project on hold for a bit, but it's there! You can click on things! And soon I'll be filling it with content: an art gallery, free shorts, blog posts, news, etceteraaaaaa.

5) I'm going to be in a couple of anthologies later in the year and early next year! How exciting! Two will be holiday themed and one is going to be a deal-with-a-demon style erotic short that I've been having a lot of fun brainstorming. More deets on that to come!

6) The brain goblins surprised me with an idea that grabbed me by the throat and has not let me have peace since. As yet unnamed, but it's a story about a political marriage between a large monster lady and a chronically ill waif of an elf prince whose people have been warring for centuries, and whose marriage is their best chance for peace. It takes place in Cillure but far in the past of ALITD. So if you like soft femdoms and subby guys who simp hard then this one's gonna be right up your alley. I'm already 21k words in despite *so many* other projects needing my attention instead.

I really hope y'all liked *Hope Like Hell!* It was a little different for me and I'm still struggling with whether or not I've managed to hit the notes I wanted to. So if you have a few minutes leaving a review on Amazon or Goodreads would really help me out!!! Every review seriously makes me so happy, even if it's not necessarily good—because someone still took the time to type something out, and even the 1 star reviews have been really respectful, proving that romance readers are the tits.

Tootles!

Miranda Sapphire, head goblin at MirandaSapphireWrites
(June 2023)

For the Curious Among You

<u>Pronunciation Guide</u>

<u>Cast</u>

    Sephyr Kasdaan (sef-FEAR KAHZ-dan)

    Eva Nadzija (AAVUH nah-JAY-yuh)

    Magdalena Nadzija (mahg-dah-LEHN-uh nah-JAY-yuh)

    Serr'eza (ser-AY-zuh)

    Naran'haa (nahr-an-HA)

    Siit'ron (SEE-trohn)

    Det. Me'Sherra Be'Lin (MAY-share-uh BAY-lihn)

    Officer Gricht (GRIKT)

    Mx. Yennya (mix yen-YUH)

    Sgt. Tuli (TOO-lee)

    Dr. Ritelak (RITE-lakk)

    Uraka (oo-ROCK-uh)

    Djelani (gel-AHN-ee)

    Dr. Shiya Vakkas (SHEE-yuh VAH-kuss)

    Krett (KREHT)

<u>Places</u>

Billieu (bill-YOO)
Exodia (ex-OH-dee-uh)

<u>Alien Races</u>
Yvrenii (i*hv-REN-ee) *short i sound, as in "in"
Felican (fell-EE-can)
Th'rak (THRAK)/Th'rakkan (THRAK-ahn)
Billieuan (bill-YOO-uhn)
Myauanni (myow-AHN-ee)

<u>Miscellaneous</u>
Vrakaash (vrah-KAHSH)/vrakaashaad (vrah-kah-SHAHD)
Pra'ja (prah-ZSA*) *as in the name Zsa Zsa Gabor

Lore

<u>Yvrenii</u>
- A rather large and imposing sentient species hailing from the Galthus Sector of Collective Space. Similar in appearance to fantasy orcs but with a third eye in between ans above the other two. Most common skin tones are green and brown, same for eye color; this is part of why Seph doesn't read as yvrenii.
- Most yvrenii serve in the vanguard at some point, pushing back against the incursion of the veshtun swarms (a large predator that operates as part of a hive mind) and protecting the civilian population.
- The yvrenii believe in the god Veldar, who is all

genders at once and the source of all life in the universe.

- Yvrenii genitals interlock tightly; in addition to a penis, males have the sleeve: an opening similar in function to a vagina but more like an anus in appearance that sits above the penis. Females have a vagina plus a prod, which is aesthetically similar to an enlarged clit and which slots into the male sleeve during heterosexual couplings. (Yes, it is cannon that the evolutionary reason for this is because early on in their species development copulation had to happen while moving to avoid predation. Why? Because it's silly and I liked it.)

<u>Billieu</u>

- Naming conventions: the surname is compounded, with "Me" prefix denoting the birth-giver and the "Be" prefix denoting the secondary parent. The suffix is always the given name of that parent.
- Billieu's thorny relationship with illness and sanitation began two generations prior to the events of the *Interstellar Attraction* series, when back-to-back pandemics ravaged the population. Some instances were airborne, others sexually transmitted, and still others genetic in nature, and the desire to avoid further damage to the population has resulted in strict laws and regulations surrounding hygiene. Clearance (with permits) must be given to live with anyone who is not immediate family. Courtships must be registered and all parties involved must be listed and given complete physicals prior to engagement in the relationship.

When courtships wish to progress into matings (i.e., marriages), additional certification obtained via genetic testing must be done, unless all parties are sterilized. Since enacting these strict measures Billieu's population and economy are recovering and experiencing fresh growth.

- This fraught relationship with illness is the reason why everyone living on Billieu and billieuans living abroad wears PPE (personal protective equipment). At the minimum they wear face masks, but may also choose to don booties, gloves, tail sheaths, or goggles.

The Intergalactic Collective

- The Intergalactic Collective of Planets, also called simply "The Collective" or "Collective Space", is the planetary alliance between the space-faring populations of known space. Contact with primitive (i.e., not yet space-faring) planets is strictly forbidden so as not to influence the evolution of primitive peoples.

Random Shit

- Most Billieuans are born with a deep cleft that goes from their hairline all the way down to their chin, kind of like the cleft in a peach.
- The helix in an intracranial implant which is wildly popular among mercenaries and others who have to work covert ops. It allows for concealment and disguise via use of a nanomesh "skin"—a "living" fabric made of nanobots that can project desired images—as well as allowing emergency comms to go out in complete silence, and activation of security systems with just a

thought. Can integrate with translation implants to boost their power and efficacy.

- Comics were not invented outside of Earth, though the female protagonist of *All or Nothing* introduces the medium to the Collective when she starts one up with her mate.

- Vrakaash was an ancient form of punishment, the origins of which are uncertain. But several centuries ago it was common practice to punish certain crimes by immersing offenders in horrifically foul cesspools filled with waste and any number of rotting things—the vrakaash pits (vrakaashaad is just the term used to indicate the person who was immersed in the pits). The pits weren't deadly or caustic, but the trauma of the experience was believed to cleanse the person's spirit of the urge to do wrong; you enter the pits full of vrakaash in your soul, and leave them having expelled that foulness into the pit. Eventually, the use of vrakaash as a form of punishment was outlawed throughout Collective Space for being too psychologically damaging and cruel.

www.ingramcontent.com/pod-product-compliance
Lightning Source LLC
Chambersburg PA
CBHW021153160726
47994CB00001B/182